# The Beauty of One's Journey

By

Maddy Grace

# Contents

# *Characters*

ZINNIA ELLIS, *an eager yet naive girl who wishes to find what it is life holds for her.*

PETER WELLS, *a charming, light-hearted stranger who ends up caring more for Zinnia than any other.*

JUNE McCAFRE, *a sweet woman who patiently shows and teaches Zinnia the way to a prosperous life, and who also proves to be the remedy to all of her problems.*

EVERIT CUMMINGS, *a handsome gentleman whose loyal companionship blossoms into love.*

ROBERT ELLIS, *Zinnia's business consumed father.*

ELOISE ELLIS, *Zinnia's frantic and hysterical mother.*

ELDA, *a caring neighbor who is tricked into being a faithful servant.*

# *Chapter I*

# *A Father's News*

One day in early April, as Zinnia Ellis was about ready to walk out the back door, her father burst in through the front.

"I did it! Eloise, I promised you I could! Now look here at such a letter and call Zinnia to see as well."

She had missed her opportunity to slip out, and now she would be forced to listen while her father rambled on about his work. He is a successful lawyer whose father died as of three years prior. This unfortunate event left Robert Ellis with around fifty-thousand dollars and a magnificent estate. Now, most people would see that this is a fine opportunity to settle down. There was more than enough money to keep him and his family out of work if spent wisely, but Robert Ellis is a man of business, whose heart is far more interested in his work than of those who live within his walls. Zinnia was soon to be called by her mother, so instead of waiting for it, she walked into the room in which her excited father occupied.

"Hurry, Eloise. Zinnia is in here," Mr. Ellis said.

Quickly and softly Mrs. Ellis came into the foyer.

"Now, I would like to be the first to tell the both of you that your father, and your husband has gotten his foot further into the door. As you both should know, I have worked very vigorously for the last few months and it has now payed off. I have been appointed the job in Elkhart. The man told me that I would be receiving almost double the clients and triple the pay. This is a big opportunity for us and I believe I am going to take it as long as it agrees with the both of you."

This news put Mrs. Ellis into a state shock. She attempted to converse, but nothing but dry breath would come from her lips. Her face was a twist between excitement and complete terror. Everyone who knows of Eloise Ellis, knows that for the better part of the time she is a hysterical mess, so her reaction to such news came as no surprise to Zinnia or her father. Zinnia was forced to ask the appropriate questions in her mother's place, and she soon found that her father was steadfast in his plan. She realized that her life would have to move on a count of her father's affairs. She never quite liked the town in which she lived, but she was certainly not ready to give it up for her father's unneeded job. This place had become accustomed to her now, after three years of living, and she was not yet ready to move from house to house for her father and his pressing job.

After her father was done with his speech and her mother was lying in bed, Zinnia went out to do what she had meant to all along. Earlier that week she had seen a quaint store on her evening walk. It piqued her interest, so she decided she might just take a look inside.

She walked out the door and through the old garden into the back roads of Corydon. The streets were of brick and looked terribly cold, while the trees seemed chilled until their leaves trembled. The wind was blustery, which made Zinnia feel that it was a rather ugly day. Just getting out of that house made her feel much better, though. The weather was extreme for the time of year. It should have been warm by this point, but it seemed the world had a different plan.

She arrived at the little place and saw that there was no light within. She decided to knock on the door. There was no answer, so she turned the knob, and surprisingly, it was unlocked.

There was an elderly woman inside, and after being startled at Zinnia's arrival, said "Oh my, I guess I didn't hear you come in," "I am so very sorry-

"No, I am sorry for interrupting you so." replied Zinnia. "I only came in to see if there was anyone here, and I now have my answer."

"Would you like to sit down, dear? I have some tea ready and it is an utmost blustery day." cooed the old woman.

"You know," replied Zinnia, "I believe that is an offer I just cannot refuse." They both chuckled lightly.

As the woman went out to fetch the tea, Zinnia decided to take a look around. When she did, she saw large bookcases with as many books as could possibly be held within them. There were pieces of intricately woven art on every wall that stood, and antiques on everyplace where they could rest. This room was oddly amusing to her. There was a smell of sweet warmth in the air and a feeling of calm interest. The woman came into the room shortly, and soon they were both settled in their chairs.

Zinnia started out by asking "So, are you the owner of this little store?"

With a friendly smile the woman replied "Why, yes. My mother and father started this store. It was a family bakery, but when the two of them passed, it was handed down to me."

"If this was a bakery, then how did you come to have so many books?" Zinnia questioned.

"Well..." the good woman answered, "I guess owning a bakery just wasn't what I was cut out for, my dear, for shortly after my owning such a store, a local library was being torn down. I simply could not stand such a thing, so I confronted the owner and asked where all of the books would be going. He supposed that there was nowhere else for them but where they lay. Now that, dearie, was on the ruins of the old library. I told that man how I felt about such a terrible deed. He said "If you feel that way, then take them yourself!" Well you better believe I did. I took every last book and piece of art off that filthy bit of earth, and then proceeded to bring them right back here. It was the only place that I had where I could store such a monstrous heap of books. I sat down on a little bench and started to work. Slowly, each of those books became new again. It must have taken me weeks to clear that pile and put them in a rightful place, but once I had, this old bakery looked mighty like a bookstore.

"No one ever paid much attention to that bakery, anyhow, once mother and father were gone. I guess they all figured that they had had enough pastries to last them a life time, and needn't buy any more. This small building became forgotten, until a gossiping-woman came in to see what in the world I was doing with all of these books. I had just had enough that day, so I told the woman "I am going to sell them, and if you please, you may buy one. But for now, I am awfully busy with my work, so if not, you may leave." Well, I guess she did what a gossiper does best, but somehow those women she spoke to were interested in my books. Soon, I had a woman come saying "I have heard of this little store from my friend Lizelle, and I came to ask if you had any children's books for my Henry." Of course, I had. I showed them to her and she was very impressed with what I had to offer. The word quickly got out about my books, and my store soon became a favorite. After a month or two, people started to not only come to buy, but also to sell, and lickety-split I was busting at the seams with people's antiques, but I like to think of them as old treasures."

"Wow…" gasped Zinnia. "What a story."

"Well, young Miss, I have many more stories to tell if you want to hear of such things."

"Oh yes, I would ma'am!" replied Zinnia. The women looked at her hard, and then falling deeper within her chair she said "Oh dear, I am afraid I have forgotten to tell you my name. Well, I am June McCafre, and what might your name be?"

"My name is Zinnia Ellis." she replied in friendly return.

"Well Zinnia, it appears to be getting quite dark-

"Oh no, I guess I lost track of time. I had better be going before my mother and father become worried." said Zinnia hurriedly.

Ms. McCafre said "Yes, my dear, I completely understand. If you would like to come again, I am nearly always here at this time. Now, you get yourself dressed proper and be on your way. Hurry now, I would not wish you to worry your parents for an old woman like me."

Zinnia put on her overcoat and scarf, then said her goodbyes and quickly went on her way.

# Chapter II

# *Zinnia Tells Her Troubles*

When Zinnia arrived at her home, she saw that their neighbor, Elda, had come over to nurse her mother back to sanity. She was a good woman for doing such a thing, and had already set herself to work in the kitchen. She appeared to be making some sort of soup and did not seem too awfully busy, so Zinnia decided to ask her if she knew where her father was.

In response Elda said "Well, I believe he went out to do business of sorts."

Zinnia quickly asked "Do you happen to know the time he will be returning?"

"No," said the sweet woman "I don't believe I do. I am utmostly sorry for my inconveniencing you, dear."

Zinnia replied "Oh, on the contrary. You have done quite more than has ever been expected to be done by a neighbor, and we shall forever be grateful." Zinnia knew that neither of her parents thought anything about what this woman had done for them, but she felt it was the least she could do to simply thank her.

Before she had left the room, Elda said "Well, I will surely have less to do, you know, with you leaving and all. It sure is a shame."

Zinnia snapped her head around, in the direction of the woman and asked in a panicked squeak "Father told you?"

"Oh, yes dear," chuckled the old woman "Why, he is so blissful, he must a' told the whole neighborhood by now!"

Zinnia fled from the room, flew up the stairs and ran down the hall until she had reached the entryway to her mother's bedroom. She struck the door twice with ever-building anxiety. With one more rap her mother pathetically said "Yes?"

Zinnia thought of the state she was in and how she must look, so she hurriedly pushed back her hair and proceeded into the bedroom. Her mother was lying there, with pillows propped and hair braided. She looked as if she had a contagious virus that could take her life at any second.

Zinnia said as calmly as could be mustered "Mother, did you happen to consent to father's job proposition?"

"Why, yes," she happily replied, "I *happen* to think it is a rather grand proposition at that." Zinnia smiled at her in an irritated way, for she knew that her mother could be easily persuaded in anyway her father wished, and in fact, already had.

Zinnia went to bed without any supper, for she could not face her father without feeling complete hatred.

He cared not of what she thought, *if* he thought of her at all.

"I have no say in where I go or what happens to me." This was the thought that was running through Zinnia's head and she could hardly bear it. She knew her life had been nothing but a mess since the time she was a child. She was now almost nineteen, and still knew nothing of what she liked. She only knew of what she hated. The girl was not a curmudgeon, and if she was thought of as one, it was only the product of the life she had been force to live since birth. She had very little to choose for herself and was always being told what to do. And yet, she was never properly taken care of. Her parents payed little attention to the well-being of their daughter, and cared not whether she be in troubles or true-hearted. A life like this can wear on a young, vibrant person like Zinnia, until it makes them dull enough to give up fighting. She had just about gotten to this point when she realized that she *would* find a way to live a life that pleased her, if only she had a foot hold.

The next morning, she arose before any of the others had a chance to blink an eye. She put on her clothes, in a hurried manner, and soon was out of the house. As she walked, the sun came up in the most beautiful of ways, and the birds chattered loudly at one another. There were many things that might have distracted one on that day, but Zinnia was not thinking of any of them. She did not start out knowing where she was headed, but she ended up at the doorstep of June McCafre's store. Luckily, there was a light coming from within, for Zinnia had no other plan but to come right to where she was.

She knocked softly on the door, for the fear of waking Ms. McCafre from her slumber, but to her surprise her knock was answered straight away with a swift call "Yes, I am here, but may I please know the name of the person standing at my door?"

Zinnia happily cried, "Oh, Ms. McCafre, it is I, Zinnia."

She then heard footsteps followed by the opening of the door. "Child, oh child, it is much too early for you to be out, for it is hardly morn. You must be frozen half to death, you get yourself in here just as soon as could possibly be expected of you!"

Zinnia scurried into the warm glow of the house. She *had* been cold, and now, after looking at her surroundings, she found that the wind was blowing at a fast and steady rate. Ms. McCafre quickly brought the girl a blanket, tea, and some sort of warm pastry. Zinnia thanked her with her heart full of gratefulness.

In a few minutes, the sweet lady sat herself down and declared "For the life of me, I cannot figure your being here,"

"I hope I did not wake you," Zinnia anxiously replied.

"Oh no, dear," Ms. McCafre said "I have been up for a long while."

Zinnia asked with much curiosity "So you live here?"

"No, I have my own house in the country," she answered, "but for some reason I just had an inkling that I should come here, and sure as day, you showed up!"

"I am sorry for disturbing you, but I just had to get out of that house of mine and as I began walking, I forgot where it was I was going. Somehow, my feet brought me here."

Ms. McCafre then said "If you would not mind my asking, dear, why would you have to run away from your home, and at this hour?"

Zinnia looked deep into the woman's eyes. She could see that there was nothing but kindness within them, so she decided to tell her.

"Well," she began "my father is a man of business and seems to care for nothing but it. From working so hard on nothing but such things, he has been given a job proposition. This deal is one that involves my family to move at least twelve counties away. Now, I have already been moved from county to county with my parent's luggage, but I have actually been able to stay in the same place ever since my grandfather's death. This is because my father received his estate and a sum of money. After my father told Mother and I about his new job, Mother nearly fainted. Do not worry yourself over her though, for she nearly always is hysterical and all who know her, know that. After she had rested and became as well as possible, Father must have come to see her, for when I saw her, she was simply wild about the idea of moving. I have now lived for eighteen long years, and yet I know not of what I like or what I want. I have no time to learn such things, for I am always being forced to do what the rest of my family pleases. I am fed up with the way my life has become, and I believe I will become awfully sick if I am forced to keep living it."

When Zinnia remembered that she was having a conversation, she quickly returned her focus on her listener.

Ms. McCafre cried "Oh, you poor child! You are safe here with me. You do not deserve to be put through such torture of the mind. You must rest until you have your bearings once again."

Zinnia then realized the stress she had put Ms. McCafre through, and said "I am so sorry for worrying you over my affairs. It was very wrong of me to do so. Please, forgive me, Ms. McCafre."

"Oh, my love, you have done nothing wrong, you merely answered my questions," said the kind woman in a soothing tone "and by my word, you are not to call me "Ms. McCafre", it sounds much too formal. We are friends now, and it is not polite to call a friend by their last name!"

Zinnia had to laugh at this fighting spirit within such a sweet woman. Then, Zinnia's eyes slowly drifted shut to the lovely sound of June reading one of her many beautiful books.

# *Chapter III*

## *June McCafre's Plan*

In the early afternoon, Zinnia awoke from a most wonderful slumber.

June quickly came to her and asked "How are you feeling, child?"

Zinnia felt livelier than she had in many years, so she replied "Ms. McCafre, I mean June, you have worked wonders. I feel so much better and my nerves have calmed remarkably. I could never repay you for all you have done for me, so I will be out of your hair, just as soon as I finish this astonishingly delicious sweet roll of yours." "Was it made from one of your family's recipe?"

June happily declared "Why yes, it sure was. I am so glad you like it!" "And Zinnia, you are not "in my hair" the slightest of a bit. I love to have you and it would make me very happy if you would stay."

"Oh, June," cried Zinnia "I would love to stay. I feel so much better when I am around you."

"Well, if you *are* to stay with me," replied June "then I will have to show you a thing or two."

"Like what?" gasped Zinnia with her brown eyes opened wide.

"Well for starters, I would like to show you my most prized possession in this store," as June said this, she walked over to a book shelf, "here we are. Now, I believe you will like this book here." "You may take it home with you. I am no longer using it and I feel that you need it a great deal more than I."

Zinnia gave June her thanks, and then carefully examined the beautiful specimen. It had a royal blue cover, with the most extraordinary markings upon it. In gold lettering it read, 'The Sun's Glory'. It seemed to be a wonderful book, with pictures, and the loveliest scrawling the girl had ever gazed upon. The book itself looked to be quite old, but she could see that it meant an awful lot to June that she read it.

"June," Zinnia started, "I could not tell you the last time I read a book. My mother and father have never promoted book reading, so I guess I never thought much about it-

"Oh," said June with a look of misunderstanding "for how young and smart you seem, I could have sworn you loved to read. It will help you a great deal in life, you know, and-

"Oh, I know June, I really should read more, and you have now helped me to see that. I promise I will read this book religiously, every night before I go to sleep. I will do anything to make you pleased with me, I know I have known you but two days, yet still I see that you are a woman of great gallantry and love. You have made me feel more joyous than I ever have in any of my childhood years, and I even feel that I know who I truly should be when I am around you. You are the most honorable person who has ever stepped foot in my life, and I simply do not know what I would do if you were to be disappointed in me. So, please correct *all* of my faults, June."

"Oh, darling," June gasped "I am not perfect enough on my own to even begin fixing others on what is true-

"If you feel that way, June, I have no right to tell you otherwise. I should have known that you are too sweet of a person to be anything but humble, but couldn't you show me your ways and tell me of the life that has made you so fine?" pleaded Zinnia.

"Well, I guess I could try, dear." chuckled June with a twinkle in her eyes.

"Tell you what, you come here around mid-morning tomorrow, and I will tell you all that could be told in one day. It would please me very much if you would tell your mother of this plan, children should always respect their parents, you know. Now, how does such a plan suit you?"

Zinnia quickly answered "Oh, it sounds simply wonderful! I am so desperate for someone good in my life and you are just the one I need. Your kindness means more to me than you will ever know, let alone the fact that you have fed and warmed me, too. Oh, and I *will* tell my mother of our plan."

"Well" June said, "you had better get going home before your folks wonder where you have gone. It is almost dinner time, and I am sure your mother has something special prepared that you should not miss."

"Oh," said Zinnia "Mother never cooks. We use to have a full time cook, but now Father has gotten our good neighbor working night and day for my mother. Mother looks so peaked, that the kind woman feels the least she could do is to stay at her side whenever needed. But you are right, I really should be on my way. I have a full day of reading to look forward to, and you still have not opened shop on my account."

With that Zinnia walked out of June McCafre's store once again. She felt very well and knew that the pendulum of life was beginning to sway in her favor, and God knows that is what she needed.

On Zinnia's arrival she heard her mother's faithful worker humming in the foyer.

"She must be dusting" thought Zinnia, but when she walked into the room, she saw her mother up and happily playing a game of cards with Elda.

Quickly her mother turned towards her. She gave a brilliant smile that would have made anyone believe that she had been well and happy most every day of her life.

"Hello, darling," said Zinnia's mother "Did you already go out for the day? My, I guessed I was too busy to notice that you had gone. Well, would you like to play a game of cards with Elda and I? You see, the game is going quite well for Elda and I could bear to restart!"

The two women started laughing until their faces turned red and they needed a drink.

"Well Mother, I *have* been out today," started Zinnia, "You see I met a very sweet woman at the bookstore, in fact she is the owner, and I was so interested in her life's story that she said I could come back tomorrow morning if it was alright with my mother. So-

"Oh, fine dear. It is good for you to get out and be social for once."

Then a storm of giggling began once again. Zinnia knew that her mother had not listened to a word she said, but it was all she could do to try for June.

When Zinnia came down from reading in the evening, she went to the kitchen to see what Elda was cooking for her hysterical mother. To her surprise her mother was in the kitchen too, and was watching with wonder at the mystical preparing of the bread.

"So, this pale sticky dough is going to make my fluffy bread?" she heard her mother ask.

Zinnia had to chuckle at this, for even though she knew very little herself, she knew her mother knew far less. For her whole life she had been worried over, so of course she did not know much of baking, cleaning, gardening, or even washing her own laundry. Zinnia walked in feeling happy. She sat by her mother at the table, and they both got a good teaching from their loyal neighbor Elda. The woman had just begun to knead the dough, when Robert Ellis came gliding through the door. He was singing with a low untuned voice, which Zinnia had learned to know, meant he was quite happy. He then proceeded to burst into the kitchen, and kiss his wife and daughter with petaled gifts in his hands.

Eloise began in astonishment "Why I never- "What on earth has gotten into you Robert? Have you gone to drinking?" she asked hotly.

"No, no, my love. I just am so happy to start our new life. I feel like a new man!"

Then he once again began singing and trouncing around the kitchen like a big buffoon. It was quite a disgraceful sight, but one, none the less, that put the whole house into an uproar of laughter. Once they were all settled and sat down to their meal, Robert began to talk of work and the stocks as usual.

"I am seeing all of my choices make this family even more money, which will help us buy a bigger house in Elkhart and start our lives off right and well." stated Robert.

Zinnia then asked "Father, do you really want to go? I know this is a big opportunity for you, but I truly do not want to leave my home to start another. I was tired of moving when we settled here, and I still am. It makes me feel ill inside, and I do not believe I can endure that pain again.  Please understand Father."

"Oh, my silly little pet, you will be fine. You are right to say that this is a big opportunity for us, it is triple the pay! You will soon get over the fact that we are leaving, for you know you take after me." said Robert in his most persuasive manner.

There was no talking to either of her parents, for when Robert Ellis has made up his mind, it is final, and when he talks of his wants to his wife in a loving way, she *wants* to believe it is final. Neither of them have ever given full attention to a word that slips from Zinnia's lips, which has taught her to simply save her breath.

# Chapter IV

# A Plan Put to Action

The next morning Zinnia arose before the sun. She could hardly bear the next few hours of waiting, but soon the time came in which she could leave. When Zinnia arrived at the old cobblestone bookstore, her nostrils were filled with the scent of cinnamon and all-spice. There was a clear view of smoke spiraling from the chimney's top, which made her mouth water at the thought of what might be baking inside.

Zinnia went to the door with ever-growing excitement. After two swift knocks, she heard June's voice call "Come in, come in. I am just finishing my apple cobbler."

Zinnia opened the old wooden door, and walked into the sweet little hut. She then quickly found the corner that June was occupying.

"Hello, my dear." June said with a smile "Are you ready for some breakfast?"

"June, you should not have gone to the trouble!" Zinnia stated "You have done quite enough as it is."

"Oh, hog-wash." June quickly answered "You wouldn't deprive an old lady of her pleasures, now would you?"

Zinnia chuckled at this stubborn old woman and answered “I guess if you put it that way, my answer can be nothing but no.”

“Good, then let’s eat.” June said. She started to plate the food and place it on the preset table. Once she sat down, Zinnia started to eat.

“Now wait just a minute,” cried June “we have not thanked the good Lord for this meal.”

“Oh” Zinnia said. “I am quite sorry. Will you say the prayer? I am afraid to admit that I do not know much about the subject.”

“That is fine dearie, you will learn.”

Then June began the prayer “Thank you Lord in heaven high, for giving me food to eat tonight. Thank you for the blessings you sprinkle in my day, thank you for giving me the power to obey. Thank you for the birds in the trees, for the flowers and for the honeybees. But most of all, thank you for my beautiful life, and for keeping me happy even through strife.”

June opened her eyes and then began to eat. Zinnia, all the while, was trying to make a mental note of the beautiful poem that she had just witnessed.

“Who taught you that prayer, June?” Zinnia asked.

“Well, my mother did.” June replied.

“What was she like?” Zinnia questioned.

"My mother? Well, she was a humble and quiet servant to the Lord. Everyone I knew thought good of her, but *my* greatest memories are the times when we would go to parties. When the fiddles would begin to play, and the people would commence to clapping, my mother would get out in the middle of the floor, and dance. She would start to twirl, ever faster, and her face would grow brighter and brighter as she did it. Everyone loved to see her dance. I swear, she danced till' the day she passed away. I only hope I will experience half as much joy in my lifetime as mother did when she danced." June stated.

She had a far off look in her eyes. Zinnia decided she was thinking of her mother and all of the memories she had of her.

Suddenly June gasped "Oh, I'm afraid I left you there for a minute. Now, what are you planning over there? I can see your mind a' working."

Zinnia said in all seriousness "June, my father loves his job, and I am glad he has something to love, but I can't help feeling that this move is the wrong thing for me."

"Well," began June "your heart will show you the true path that your mind cannot comprehend. Maybe you should think less, and listen to what your conscience is truly telling you. If you still feel that it is wrong to leave, then tell your parents so."

"Oh, I've tried! They simply will not listen!" cried Zinnia "But I was thinking, I am nearing nineteen and could be of great help to you if you would teach me. Mother and

Father care not where I go or what happens to me, but I do, and I feel that the best place for me is with you."

June was baffled at this remark. She thought for a while, then said "I will go see your mother and talk to her of this matter. I will see where she stands and how she acts towards you. Now let's go. I have a cake that I can bring her anyhow."

Zinnia showed June the way to her father's estate. As they walked, June talked of the beauty she saw, and Zinnia started to see it for the first time. Once they arrived at the house, they knocked on the door. There was a voice from the kitchen saying "Come in Zinnia, for this is your own house!" Then they heard laughter come from the speaker.

"That is the neighbor I told you of." Zinnia said.

They walked through the door.

June looked around at the magnificent building in shock "Why, I never," she began.

After looking through a few rooms for her mother, Zinnia saw her sitting at a desk in the picture room.

"Mother," she exclaimed, "I brought my dear friend, Ms. June McCafre, with me. I wanted you both to meet."

"Hello," said Eloise in a very elegant manner, "It pleases me to make your acquaintance."

"No, no, it really is my pleasure," June began, "you see, your daughter has come and visited with me at my store for the last few days. She truly is a doll. We got to talking and Zinnia told me that she would like us to meet, so naturally I agreed to the invitation to visit with the woman who has raised such a fine daughter."

"Why, it pleases me that my daughter is thought of in such a way. Would you like some tea? My good friend is making me some at the moment, and I am sure that there is plenty for you."

"That would be quite nice, that is if you are sure of it's being no trouble." June answered courteously.

"No trouble at all." grinned Eloise. She rang her bell for Elda, and out she came from behind the kitchen door. Zinnia knew she must have been listening in, for she had nothing better to do with her day. Eloise started to tell her of the extra cup of tea that was needed, but before she finished Elda dashed into the kitchen.

"Well," began June, "I hear that you are moving away."

"Oh, yes" said Eloise excitedly, "my husband and I have it all worked out. We plan to leave at the end of the week."

Zinnia butted in, "Mother, you never told me of this. I do not wish to leave, not now that I have found such a wonderful friend to aspire to. You see, June is the owner of a bookstore, she lives a life that appeals to me and I wish to learn from her,"

Elda then hurried back into the room with the hot tea and some muffins, as if she did not want to miss another word.

June began to speak, so all listened "You see I actually came here to see you, over this matter. I am growing older, and there is still ample work that cannot be ignored. It would be beneficial for me to have some help. I have taken to your daughter with great love, and I believe that if I were allowed to help her learn the skills of my knowledge, that it would help the both of us. Me with my work, and her with her life. And that is why I came; to talk to you and your husband, and see if Zinnia could be my apprentice for a while. She seems very eager to learn, and it truly would be a great joy to pass on my knowledge."

"Why," stuttered Eloise, "I do not know what to say about this. I am glad that my daughter has finally taken interest in something, but I would need to discuss it with my husband first."

"Of course," June agreed.

"What did you say your name was, again?" asked Eloise.

"I am June McCafre." June stated.

"And you own a bookstore?" questioned Eloise.

"Yes, I do." June replied "It is located on Fox Street on the outskirts of town."

"Near the bakery?" said Eloise.

"No, but it once was a bakery, my mother and father were the owners. I worked there as a young adult." June answered.

"You know," Eloise said with her face starting to glow "I remember going there once with my mother. I was only a child, but I remember a young girl was working. She had a red tint to her hair, and a smile that made you feel wonderful. I believe you are her."

"Why, what a funny coincidence." laughed June.

"I no longer believe; I know it was you!" stated Eloise.

With that, they began to talk as if they had been friends for years. It was a wonderful occasion. Everything was well and gay within that room. The women laughed for hours and told grand stories, and for once, the house felt more like a home.

Just as one of the stories were being finished, in waltzed Robert. He had a surprised look on his face.

He came over and kissed his wife, then said "Hello, who might you be?"

"I, sir," answered June with great respect, "am June McCafre. I am a friend of Zinnia's."

"Oh," exclaimed Zinnia's father "it is a pleasure to meet you Mrs. McCafre. May I join your conversation?"

"You most certainly may." answered June.

"Yes, dear, we would love you to." Eloise added, "June came here to meet us, but then I realized that I had met her when I was but a small child. We have since talked through the whole day, and have had a ball. I know you will just love her! I was thinking we might play cards tonight, before supper. Would that suit you, love?"

"Yes, I believe a good game of cards would be delightful. I will go change into more suitable attire, and be down promptly."

Robert jogged upstairs. The women grew loud enough that their giggling could be heard from the second story. When he came back down, the cards were on the table, and set to play. He took the seat that had been appointed to him, and gladly began to play.

They all had a jolly good time, and even Elda was invited into the game. By the end of the night, they all were red and exhausted from laughter.

Then Eloise said "You see, dear, sweet Mrs. McCafre came over to ask if Zinnia could be her apprentice for a while. She told me that she would teach her of her trade, and of all that is important in life. We could go off to Elkhart, none the less, it would be a sort of honeymoon. Zinnia is just dying to go with June, and you know how she hates to travel."

"Well," exclaimed Robert with his face twisted in thought "I guess that would be fine."

He then began to smile, as if a growing idea was swelling inside him.

"It should not interfere with our plans in the least. Yes, darling, you and I can go up to Elkhart and get our lives settled there, and June can send us a message when the time is right for our daughter to join us. I would be happy for such a grand woman to teach our daughter, it would help her a great deal,"

"Oh, thank you, Father!" Zinnia excitedly squealed.

"Do not thank me, thank Mrs. McCafre. I am sure you two will have a marvelous time, and it will be much easier on your mother and I as well. I was dreading the thought of having to drag you, kicking and screaming, to Elkhart. I know how you hated the idea of the move."

"Father, I assure you," stated Zinnia "this is the best thing you could ever do for me. And I *am* forever grateful to you, June, for this wonderful arrangement. It means everything to me, thank you."

"Oh, it is my pleasure." said June. "If it is no trouble for you, I will take Zinnia in four days' time, that is when you are leaving, is it not?"

"Yes, yes indeed." cried Eloise, who had been acting like a little child who wanted to do everything in her power to please June.

"That will suit us fine." Robert answered.

"Good, you all may drive over to my house, and see if it is suitable for the girl. If you find it to be well, then you may drop her off and be on your way." June said.

She then continued to write down her address on a bit of paper, and hand it to Eloise. With a grin of her eyes, June left with their promises to soon come and see her.

After she left, Robert was happier than ever. He was acting like a puzzled child himself. He would sputter and wonder at that June McCafre, and then chuckle. Robert went on like this for a good while. He talked of how wise a woman she was, and how happy he was to leave his daughter with such a lady.

At last, all was well in Zinnia's heart. The dust had begun to settle, and she would be off to June's house in only a few more days. These where the thoughts that drifted through the girl's head as she fell asleep with June's book in her lap.

# Chapter V

# *The Carriage Ride*

The days that were left before her parent's trip were spent packing and planning with great excitement. All three of them had smiles that would not cease, and happy hearts for the adventure at hand. Those four days flew by, heavy with things to do. Finally, the time came in which to leave their old house and take Zinnia to June's. The small family piled into their carriage, yet found it to be a tight fit. This was due to the face that it was not only them in this carriage, but also all of their earthly belongings. The team was drawn from the stables and brought to their heavy load.

Robert said "I am not sure if these poor old horses can carry all of these things."

Sure enough, they did, but very slowly.

The family set off to the address that June had given them. They drove around for an hour or so, until they finally came to a woods. There they had to drive along a road tracing this dense forest. After getting half way around the perimeter, there was a small dirt path in which they were to follow. At this, Robert began to question the directions he was given, but after a quick dispute it was decided to carry on in the direction of the small trail.

Along this trail there were trees towering high above on either side, Zinnia could tell by the size of them that they had been there for many years before she was ever born. There were little birds in the trees and in every brier bush. When you looked hard through the lines of trees you could see a deep green pasture. There seemed to be bright spots here and there. At first Zinnia could not identify what exactly they were, but she then came to the conclusion that they must be wildflowers.

She turned to her mother and saw the look of confusion and awe upon her face, just as was on her own. It truly was magnificent there. The day itself was much better than the last, for the earth had begun to warm and everything was growing.

After riding on this overgrown path for what seemed to be a great while, the family finally came to a clearing. A tall line of rosebushes was seen first, to be sure. The carriage passed this perfumed mass, and to the family's surprise, there were many amazing hidden flowers to be seen behind it. A barn came into view to the left, and then a shed. It went on like this until they made it to a little, fresh house. This house was in fact more like a cottage. It was painted a dull, dusty shade of blue that reminded Zinnia of slate. Each barn and chicken house had an unmatched color to the home. There were reds, greens, and whites, but somehow, they all worked together to bring a feeling of home.

"My, I have never in my life seen anything like it," gasped Robert.

"To be sure, dear." gasped Eloise in reply.

Zinnia gave no comment, for she was taking in all of the beauty that was to now be her life. The gardens were already planted, and flowers all around where in bloom. It was a fantasy, a fantasy hidden in a dark green, untouched woods. The carriage was stopped, and the family piled out of it. There were soon suitcases to be hauled and bags to be taken.

Hearing all the commotion, June stepped out of her house and exclaimed "Why I'll be drawn on, do all these things come with you?"

She was gesturing to Zinnia, who looked around at the mess of things she had acquired.

"Why yes, of course they do." said Zinnia matter-of-factly.

For though Zinnia thought this was what she wanted, and it very well may be, she was still a girl with a sheltered life from the city, with no idea of how to do anything for herself. June saw this, and began to realize the kind of work that was cut out for her.

# *Chapter VI*

# *A Quick Investigation*

Once the Ellis's had all of Zinnia's things piled on the front porch, June began to show them where their daughter would be staying. When they first walked through the door, they came into the kitchen. Here there were lovely white-painted board walls. There were many small cabinets as well, and a little pantry. On the rafters there were dried flowers and herbs strung about to prolong the harvest from the year prior.

"This is quite small. Is it not for you, June?" asked Robert.

"Why, it is not small at all for me. I am sure it seems to be to you, but I believe that two people can live quite happily and comfortably with very little space." replied June.

"I believe you are right, and if you do not mind, then neither do we." Eloise added.

"I like it." Zinnia stated "You have a very nice house, and I would be happy to call it my home."

"That is good, my dear." June said approvingly.

Then the guide and her guest moved into the next room, which just so happened to be the parlor. Zinnia noticed that every piece of furniture that filled this room was exclusively wooden, just as the last room had been. They all seemed to be home-made, for the girl had never seen anything like them before. The parlor had large windows looking out over the gardens, and beautiful paintings strewn through-out the room.

The family proceeded to looking through the small house. There were only three bedrooms left to see, they were all terribly old and not nearly as magnificent as the ones back at her home, yet still Zinnia remained perfectly oblivious to this fact. Although June's house did not have the newest things within, it was still kept up and watched after. This place was very peaceful, you could tell much love had been given to all that was inside. Therefore, all that looked through the house that day, knew that it meant very much to June.

June took Robert and Eloise outside and showed them her gardens. While they were doing this Zinnia took her things inside and began to unpack, for her parents said it was very suitable and she might as well begin the process. Everywhere June took them, the pair were in shock. She showed them the barns, the animals, and all of the beautiful things she had.

Once the tour had ended, June went inside and made some iced tea and lemonade. This was because the day had begun to warm and after all, the Ellis's were not use to so much walking. They then sat on the porch, and talked the afternoon away.

June asked "So, Zinnia, do you think you *would* like to stay?"

"Yes, of course." Zinnia answered promptly "I am already unpacked."

"Well, this will be a big change for you, but I am sure we will get along just fine." said June in a cheery voice.

"Why, I believe you are a very lucky girl, Zinnia, for being able to have such a fine experience. You know I never liked country life, but I am glad that you are strong enough to peruse it. I did not think you had it in you." Eloise said. It seemed she had a way of making even a complement sound condescending.

"Well, I believe we must be going, dear." stated Robert.

"Yes, we did expect to have been going by now." answered Eloise in a voice that told she had forgotten all about their prior plans.

With that, the excited couple took off on their journey with no whining daughter to care for. Things seemed to have worked out splendidly. Zinnia promised to write, and so did her mother. They gave hurried kisses and hugs, then as quick as a rabbit, her parents were gone.

# Chapter VII

# The First Meal

Zinnia watched as her parents flew down the dirt trail. Then she excitedly turned to June. "So," she began "what are we to do first?"

June gave a twinkling grin and said "I am mighty hungry, so I am going to start fixing dinner."

With that, the old woman got up and walked into the house. Zinnia nearly ran after her, with very little control over her actions. Once they reached the kitchen she asked "May I help any?"

"Of course, you are to help!" cried June "Won't you be kind enough to remember that working is how you will be earning your stay. I have hired myself as your teacher, so that is precisely what I will be doing you silly goose!" laughed June.

This cleared the air and made Zinnia stop herself from forgetting all of her manners. She attempted to calm herself and proceeded to ask "What may I help you with first?"

"Well, you can start by helping me peel and slice potatoes. I think that is what we will be having, that is if you like fried potatoes." said June.

“I do not believe I have ever tried them.” answered Zinnia.

“Why, we can’t have that, my dear. That is exactly what I’ll fix then! Maybe with a side of cooked carrots and canned green beans.” With that June began flying about the kitchen. “Of course, we must have bread with honey and jam.” June stated in a way that let Zinnia know she had begun talking to herself.

She took a few potatoes from the pantry, and set them on the counter. Then, happily began showing Zinnia how she was to peel them. It took June a matter of seconds to peel a potato, but when Zinnia tried her hand at it, she was indeed much slower. In fact, she only had half of her peel off before June had finished the rest of the spuds. The girl had cut her fingers, and they were steadily dripping pure red. This worried Zinnia for she truly had never gotten cut or scratched many times in her life. June assured her that it would be fine, and took care of her with a motherly heart.

“I believe you had better watch me for a time before you go headlong into things.” June then encouragingly added “But do not worry, for you will soon be better equipped than I for most anything life throws at you.” This kept Zinnia’s spirits up, and her eyes constantly on June’s deft hands.

Soon, dinner was prepared and set on a lovely maple table, which was embellished with many little scrolls and notches of varying shapes and sizes. It was fairly simple, yet of great beauty. Checkered fabric of the lightest yellow had been made into placemats for each seat around the table. Upon them lay delicate, old china, shining brightly with glaze. Each plate had a different scene painted upon it's cheery face. Some of spring fields and others of winter's frozen lakes. Every cup had interestingly shaped glass, all of a separate color. The particular vessel that stood before Zinnia was of blue glass, a shade that even she had never seen before. In the center of this setting, towered a tall vase of flowers. At the end of each stretching stem sat a smiling head of petals, each fighting for their face to be seen for they knew that they were prettiest. The food itself wafted its tempting scent throughout the house. There was homemade bread, strawberry jam, apple cider, and many other delightful things surrounding the hungry pair.

June finally sat down at the table and began her favorite prayer "Thank you Lord in heaven high, for giving us food to eat tonight. Thank you for the blessings you sprinkle in my day, thank you for giving me the power to obey. Thank you for the birds in the trees, and the flowers and the honeybees. But, most of all, thank you for my beautiful life, and for keeping me happy even through strife,"

Zinnia then opened her eyes for she thought June had finished, but after looking up she saw June's eyes were still tightly shut. June then began once again, "And thank you for Zinnia, the wonderful girl who you have sent to me. Help me to show her what is good and well, and please, Father, help her to see the world that she has not yet discovered. Bless her with all of Your heart, and I shall do the same."

With that, June was finished. She began to dish herself and Zinnia's plate. With no chatter from Zinnia, June decided to look and see what was occupying her. To the woman's surprise, Zinnia's eyes were filling with large glossy tears.

"Oh darling, whatever is the matter!" gasped June in a horrified shriek. She was instantly up and at Zinnia's side, petting her hair and drying her eyes with the corner of her apron. "Are you sick, do you miss your parents, shall I call for them,"

"No," said Zinnia "it was only that in your prayer you included me and spoke such lovely things toward my future. My family has never bestowed such a love towards God and others in my whole life as you have in a mere few days. If God blesses as readily as you believe He does, I just know He has blessed you in all you ever have done."

"Oh, why thank you for saying such a thing." replied June but then she quickly asked with great concern "Are you sure you are not feeling ill?"

"I am just fine, thank you. I believe we should eat this wonderful meal that you have prepared for us, before it goes cold." answered Zinnia with ever-growing happiness shinning upon her face.

The potatoes were of golden brown, and had a taste that never tired. The bread tasted like honey itself, with nothing on it, but with the jam, it tasted like an elegant dessert fit for a queen. Just the aroma of such bread was better than any that faithful Elda had made at Zinnia's home. The cider was sweet and made your heart warm with its spicy fragrance. The dessert was a fine custard. Each scoop in the bowl was a perfect sphere, drizzled in an auburn syrup and topped with luscious wild blackberries. This meal was one to be remembered, and in its altogether perfectness, I do not believe it possibly could have been forgotten.

After they had finished their dinner, June began to clean the table. Zinnia helped by bringing dishes to the sink, but when it came time to wash them, she was in for a great shock. "Do you mean to tell me that you wash the dishes yourself!" she asked with grand emotion.

"Why, of course." laughed June.

"And you wash them after every meal!" Zinnia asked in amazement.

"Yes, I do." June looked at Zinnia with a questioning face "I take it your mother never did her own dishes, and neither have you." she pausing to read Zinnia's flabbergasted face, and then continued "Well, better late than never! You will learn today."

June took Zinnia by the arm and showed her to the sink. It took great patience, but after reassuring Zinnia that many people do, in fact, do their own dishes, she learned quite readily.

"You are a true lady, June," Zinnia said as she was drying the sparkling dishes "and if you can do the dishes, then I very well should!"

With that, Zinnia was restored with new self-confidence. She began to steadily work. After finding joy in the little sudsy bubbles and her reflection in the shining glass, the work was soon done and she felt much better for it.

# *Chapter VIII*

## *Worries Began to Fade*

"Well," breathed June "would you like to see what your new home consists of?"

"Oh, yes!" cried Zinnia happily "I have been waiting with all of the patience I could muster. I nearly would rather die than to not see such a lovely homestead as this!" With that, they walked out of doors to see the lay of the land, as well as what lay upon it. The first thing in their vision was a flower garden of every color in the Creator's pallet.

On this mid-April noon, the air was refreshing and warming, it would be impossible not to notice the glory of all creation within that day. To walk into the garden, they had to pass beneath a short corridor of wisteria vines. The pergola, which held up these vines was of strong, white colored wood. There were intricately sculped buttresses at each corner that had birds, and many other delightful things of vibrant color painted upon them. There were slabs of thin river rock laid thoughtfully about, in place of walkways. On either side of these improvised paths, every beauty of the month was in bloom. Such as, the delicate crocus of purest purple, the yellow of the daffodil's ruffled skirt, and only here could every rich colored tulip be found with its face kissing God. If you followed these paths to their very end, you would find that they all adjoined at one beauteous pond. This pond looked like a large piece of pottery. It was above ground and ran like a canal, fitting in naturally with the wall of flowers behind it. To the left of this pond there was a wheel, which appeared to be cycling water just as a mill would. There must have been a creek running nearby which fed such a contraption. The sound of it was delightful. There, under the spraying water, little spotted fish swam about. They would dart in groups around their mother, then dash back to the wheel, obviously in the midst of some fascinating game. There were large water lilies within this clear glass, some of a faint pink, that lay elegantly upon floating leaves, and others of glowing white, which smiled brightly above the surface. The seats surrounding this lovely show, sat there as to allow one to watch butterflies that glided down from the heavens, hear the chirping of the song sparrow's chicks, and smell the sweet fragrance of the perfect garden.

At such a place June and Zinnia sat. It seemed as if they were in a hidden room of unfailing magic. Everything was simply perfect. Zinnia loved to watch the little fish swimming to and fro, and was amazed at how many new sights there were to be seen.

"My, what a lovely flower that is." Zinnia gasped as she gazed upon a steadily opening bloom.

"Yes, that is one of my favorites," declared June "it is called a crocus. They are the very first flower in my garden to show their face after winter's storms, and they always bring such good news."

"Oh," Zinnia replied ignorantly "what news is it that they bring?"

"Why, they act as a messenger for the other flowers by telling us of their soon coming arrival, but also of the good weather that must follow them." June answered with her face glowing pure joy, and her lips and cheeks blazing a charming hue of pink. She was a perfect image of womanhood. Just to think that life could be even more splendid than it was at that sanctified moment, left the two of them full of bliss and excitement for the coming season.

They left the "Garden of Grandeur" as Zinnia described it, and proceeded to the potting shed. This was a small room with a little wooden table. All around the room there were terracotta pots and tin watering cans. Tools of every sort were strewn about, proving to Zinnia what work lied ahead.

Next, they examined the chicken house. Many odd things were to be seen there for sure, especially for someone who is not used to farm life. The hens clucked and feathers flew. If one could decipher their talking, it most definitely would consist of nearly all gossip, for no other sort of talk had the tone in which those hens chattered. Zinnia did not find much enjoyment in them, to tell honestly, this was because she was a little shy around animals. She never did have any of her own, for she lived in the city within the clenches of high-society's ideals, which had very little appreciation for wildlife.

Then at the back of the house, they went to the vegetable garden. Here, they found a few things planted. In Zinnia's mind it seemed as if there were hundreds of little plants sprouting among the earth, and indeed there were, but to June it was merely a few seeds that could withstand the bitterness of the changing weather. She told Zinnia of how there were many more seeds to plant, and how those sprouts were not even a quarter of the garden. Zinnia nearly fainted at the thought of the whole garden, which looked to her as big as a field, planted with green ferny vegetables. All that work would be nearly enough to make a brawny man fall to the ground with exhaustion, how in the world could this time-honored woman do it?

To the left of the cottage, about eighty feet, there was a gorgeous red barn. It sat handsomely upon a hill with a lone white oak tree standing gallantly beside it. Before you even got to the doors, you could see the white stripes outlining them. After the long hike to the top, June opened these doors. They hastily revealed what it was they enclosed, which was a golden room of sunshine that was abundantly pouring in through the hayloft above. Immediately, there could be detected the strong sweet odor of hay drifting about. After their eyes were adjusted, a long line of stables could be seen. There was a straight dirt path running from one end to the other of the barn.

June then said "In this barn, I keep my milking cows, team of horses, sheep herd, ducks, geese, and a few barn cats. They are a lot to feed and take care of on my own, so I just know having you here to help will lessen the chore considerably." June stated gladly.

"I just cannot fathom how it is you went about taking care of them all alone for as long as you have." replied Zinnia in awe "I do hope I *can* help. I know nothing about animals, and I really have never taken the time to observe them. I *am* ready to learn though."

"Well," replied June "That is good enough for me." They proceeded down the middle of the barn, June explaining things all the way. "Here," she said "is where I keep the saddles, bridles, brushes, carts, and other things for the animals."

"I did not know that you had to brush the animals." Zinnia commented.

"My, but they do love to be brushed." replied June "The horses will start loudly protesting if you don't give them a gentle brushing every now and again."

"Oh." Zinnia said, now with slightly more understanding.

They went up the ladder to the hayloft, there Zinnia saw a flash of calico before her. The cat quickly fled from the face of an unknown stranger. When Zinnia asked about the cat, she assumed it was a male, but after reconfirming that she saw calico, June told her it was a female.

"How can you tell so quickly, June?" questioned the unknowing girl.

"Well, to my knowledge every calico cat *is* a female. If you ever find one that is a male, you run straight to me, because a calico of that gender has not yet been discovered." answered June in a gentle way.

"How, in heaven's name, do you know all you do!" cried Zinnia in surprise "There are so many things that I am evidently clueless about, yet you seem to hold every answer!"

"Oh no, on the contrary. I only know of what I have seen here on the farm. The only one who holds all of the answers is the all-powerful Creator, and mark my words, that's a fact!" Zinnia did as she was told. Then she simply had to laughed at the steadfast ways of the pleasant life-worn woman standing in front of her, and what a woman she was, at that.

Once the pair reached the ground again, they walked on the dirt floor to the barns end. There was a gate that lead to a bountiful pasture, where all the animals previously talked of were grazing. Dandelions were growing and the bees were blithesomely enjoying their sweet yellow nectar. The cows had their young, wabbly legged calves basking and rolling in the warm grass beside them. They were woolly and had big kind eyes, just as most black angus do. The ducks and geese were wading in a small pond that was deeply planted within a valley. It seemed, on their roster, intently caring and mothering over their eggs, preening, and bathing was what came first. How funny they did seem, with the way they waddled and squawked at one another. The little lambs were of such pure white that they seemed holy. They happily fed off of their mother's milk and played freely under the supervision of a protecting nearby ram. Lastly, the graceful horses were seen grazing in their own secluded pack. They had colors of gray, blonde, brown, and white with black specks. There were one of each, and all were equally lovely. There were a few foals frolicking about, which were to be sold to a neighbor who needed them. They were so beautiful; it truly was a pity.

After exiting the barn, June lead Zinnia back down the hill and to her front porch. There they sat on a hanging, white wicker swing, and talked things over. The sun was rapidly falling and had now beginning to hug the western-most sky, causing the clouds to turn colors of purple, orange, and pink.

"I never, even in all my life of travel through cities and towns, have ever seen such a wonderous place as this. So many things are happening, and all in unison. There are many things growing and living off of your land, just as you always have and I very soon shall be. There is so much beauty, I hardly think I can take it all in." Zinnia said wistfully.

"My, but you do have plenty of time to make it ever-lasting. Whether in my vision, mind, or heart, this land is always with me." June dreamily replied.

Zinnia looked all around at the earth she had previously dwelt upon. She took a deep sigh of relief, for the thought of being a deprived, impudent girl was no longer upon her. She had cleared the chalk which cluttered her slate, and was soon to draw a new rapturous picture in place of it.

# Chapter IX

# *The First Night*

After their pleasant talk, Zinnia and June decided to go inside and enjoy the delicious meal that was readily prepared. It was of just as much grandeur as the last but with much more color and varying flavors. As the main course there was baked chicken, accompanied by mashed potatoes, gravy, caramelized carrots, canned peaches, and apple cobbler. There was enough food presented to feed a whole gang of hungry, tired lumbermen, yet the two ladies bravely endured the meal with enough room for their dessert.

Once the meal was finished and the dishes cleaned, June went about the house lighting her lamps. When she was finished each room was brightly lit and smiling convincingly with warmth, though the brisk night air proved otherwise. June noticed this, so she cheerfully went out into the dark to gather wood for the fire.

"My," gasped Zinnia "are you not afraid to go out at this hour?"

"Why, of course not." replied June "What have I to be afraid of? In all my years of living, I have never once found a thing that proves ugly enough to be feared. Fear is just a silly old thing anyhow, for the only things we truly *do* fear, are the things we do not know of. Now, I have lived long enough to know, that in fact, I know very little, but I have made up my mind to be excited for the unknown, and that is precisely what I shall continue to think. In my way of thinking, this is a much better way to live then growing suspicious over every shadow and growing more frightened through-out each day."

"I suppose you are right," shuttered Zinnia "but after all, it is only human-nature to be weary of the dark creeping things."

"Yes dear, I know." June sweetly replied "If it bothers you to go out at night, then you just sit yourself down and..."

"No thank you, June. This is a new chapter of my life. I will not allow myself to live in fear any longer. Let us go get that wood!"

With that Zinnia proudly walked out the front door and into the dark, cloudy night. But right where she stood her fearlessness stopped, and she was then left alone with her old shuttering self. June was following Zinnia, but after seeing her sudden stop, she walked right past her and affectionately grabbed hold of her hand. Together they walked to the woodshed. All the way Zinnia looked around, jumping at every little noise she heard. Then it came time for her to carry the wood. June attempted to put a piece in Zinnia's arms, but at this action Zinnia shrieked and down crashed the wood to the old dirt floor. June patiently picked up the log that had fallen and said "It was only me, child. Do not be frightened." Zinnia did not reply, but instead took a log from where she had seen June get the last. Then they both headed back towards the house.

June put her arm full into the iron wood box, and Zinnia put in her piece, which was no larger than a fallen stick from the yard, in as well. June swept back out the door and Zinnia hastily followed, being too frightened to stay alone. They got their load, and after June saw how hard that small trip was for the dainty, pampered girl, she decided to call it enough. Zinnia sank into a nearby chair and stared into the fireplace as June ignited the paper which set the kindling to flames.

"I will make us some tea." June promptly stated after the fire was tended. She went to the nearby kitchen and continued "I know that was not exactly what you are used to, but you will soon grow accustom to the darkness and will think no more of it than you do in the day. I am quite proud of you Zinnia; you have done very well for your first day."

"Now June, you know what you say is untruthful. I have failed at the few things I have attempted, and that was very little..."

"Oh, non-sense, child. I always say, "just like a flower, you cannot bloom in every season. You will learn in due time. I have no doubt about it." June said in her own matter-a-fact way.

Soon, after drinking June's tea, Zinnia's cold, white cheeks began to glow a brilliant crimson. Her heart was again full, all anguish had passed, and hope was restored.

Jolly conversation filled the room as the pair talked over details of their past and future plans.

"I would like to know what makes up this tea. Nothing Mother has ever boughten tastes similar to this spice."

"That would probably be because I made the mixture myself. I saved and dried the mint leaves from my own kitchen garden and I foraged the wild ginger near a pond within the woods. The ginger will only grow there, you see, for the ground around the pond has the exact conditions to encourage such flavor."

"I would love to see them growing in the wild someday."

"Oh, you most definitely shall. I will show you all around my woods, if you wish to see it. It is as much my heart as this farm. My, but isn't it getting late. Let me show you to your room and get you settled."

"I guess you are right, it has gotten rather late, hasn't it? Oh, and I would just love to see my room, thank you."

With that they traveled upstairs, June in the lead as always. She took a left turn at the top of the staircase; this was Zinnia's new room. It was hard to see at that time of night, but there could be distinguished large flowers upon the walls. A washing bowl and pitcher set atop a wooden vanity, and a mirror was hung on the wall behind it. But this mirror appeared almost black from the hazy midnight sky lurking outside the window. There were two lamps in which to give light, but despite their efforts, they seemed to do very little. There was darkness at three out of the four corners in the room, but still Zinnia could see large silhouettes of furniture lining the walls. It was a small room, yet suitable. It is safe to say, though, that Zinnia was very much accustom to a quite different way of living. In fact, her room at home was about four times as large as the one she was now to inhabit.

June was cheerful, as per usual, and happily told Zinnia where a few things were if she happened to need them. "Your bag is there on the vanity chair. After you get dressed for bed, you can find water within the pitcher that is setting upon the table, there," June said gesturing towards where one of the warm lights sat "which you may use to bathe your face and brush your teeth. I hope you will be happy here, and find a peaceful rest."

"Thank you once again, June, for all you have done to help me. I truly needed you and there you were with open arms and an open heart. You shall never know how much you have comforted me."

"My, but you are all wrong, dear, you are the one who has comforted me. Never has my house felt so full, nor have my rooms sounded so merry. I truly thank you. Have good dreams now." June lovingly cooed.

"Oh, I will!" Zinnia laughed gleefully.

Then, June left the room and lightly closed the door behind her. Zinnia felt a little weary of all the unknown shadows that were cast upon the floor, but she quickly remembered what June had told her about fear and how silly it truly was. This forced Zinnia to try to keep a strong front, and dismiss the thoughts that came to mind. After, dressing, and brushing her hair and teeth, Zinnia peeled back the covers on the unfamiliar bed. She laid down, and to her surprise, found it quite comfortable. Then the tension that had grown with her excursion through the darkness was soon relieved by a peaceful and revitalizing sleep.

# <u>*Chapter X*</u>

# *Tricks of the Trade*

Zinnia awoke the next morning to the sound and smell of cooking from the kitchen below. Her eyes fluttered until she final came to consciousness. Zinnia sat up in her bed, rubbed her eyes, then suddenly remembered were she was. She curiously looked around the unfamiliar room, for the sun was now shining, which made objects much more apparent than they were the night prior. There was a standing wardrobe sitting in front of her bed with birds and flowers carved into the corners. A night table stood nearest the window, looking very stout with its thick legs and wide drawers. The wallpaper was of faint pink with plate sized roses scattered about it.

Zinnia, while getting out of bed, found the vanity to be even more lovely than she had thought. It matched the wardrobe, with its dark cherry color, but the engravements were of much more delicately. There were four drawers, each having a scene from a different season. All were tastefully crafted, each so realistic that you felt as if you yourself were within the drawer's season. The desk itself was quite simple, with its smooth top and rounded corners. It did open, however, to reveal a hiding place for the most valuable of jewelry. The mirror towering above, was framed by carvings of large oak trees and barn swallows that flew about the sky. This made it so when you looked into the mirror, you saw yourself within a dense forest of merry little creatures.

The enchanted girl hurriedly got dressed and ready for the day. She felt as if she were a child on Christmas morning, as she quickly fled down the stairs in pursuit of the smell of cooking food. She ended up in the kitchen, were June was preparing breakfast.

"Oh, there you are. I was not sure how long you would sleep, but I figured on you waking soon, so I decided to start breakfast. How did you sleep?" asked June.

Zinnia had not thought of this in her hurry that morning, but after she had, she found that she did have a great night's rest.

"I slept wonderfully. How long have you been up?" inquired Zinnia.

"Well, let's see," June said while flipping a pancake and scrambling eggs "probably an hour or two." she finished nonchalantly.

A chair was pulled out in front of where Zinnia stood, but instead of taking it she asked if she could help. June respectfully declined her offer by saying "...there will be many chores after breakfast for you to help with, and I don't want you too tuckered out on your first day. Why don't you just let me finish this up, and you can do plenty of the work after."

Zinnia agreed for she knew that she was no good at cooking. They ate a hardy breakfast of fried potatoes, scrambled eggs, pancakes, and sausage. After they had finished, they each put on one of June's overcoats, for Zinnia had no sufficient clothing of her own to work in. Then the two of them set out together to do the morning chores.

First, the pair entered the chicken coop to feed those old gossiping hens. June masterly demonstrated all that Zinnia was to do. The food was to be measured out into a pail, so that the chickens were not under or over fed, then the pail was dumped evenly into bowls so that each chicken had an even chance at her food. There was a rooster in the back of the coop, secluded from the rest, soon Zinnia found out why, for when she timidly dropped his dish in, the mean thing ran around and crowed till her ears nearly split, then attacked the dish. June told Zinnia of how he did not take kindly to humans and would nearly demolish your hand if you were not careful. Then she quickly added, after seeing the girl's eyes grow large with terror, that he was nothing to be feared while he was safely caged away. This, of course, was not Zinnia's favorite job, but she had come there to work so that was exactly what she aimed to do.

Next, they walked up the lofty hill to the big red barn. June told Zinnia as she went of how the wheel barrel at the end of the barn was to be gotten, and then put below the ladder that led to the hayloft. Zinnia proceeded to do as she was instructed. Though when they both went up the hayloft with pitch forks in hand, and June started pitching the hay over the edge and into the barrel, Zinnia got a thorough shock. She somberly began her chore, and was soon convinced that the hardest she had thought it would have been, was a mere joke to what it really was. Perspiration beaded down Zinnia's temples and many curls strayed from her neatly done hair. Just when she thought she could take no more, June said "All right, I believe that is enough." Back down the ladder they went, and then back to where they had gotten the wheel barrel. There June gathered four or five different bags, each surely weighing twenty pounds, and loaded them in with the hay. The barrel was now full, and heading back down the line of stables. Each animal was in their proper place impatiently awaiting their late breakfast.

"Now," June said "we give each of my lovely pets their meal. Let's start with the cows..."

And so, the spry old woman and the nearly exhausted young lady went about giving each animal their feed. There were so many directions, that Zinnia's head began to whirl as she tried to remember what grain was for which animal and how much she was to give them. Though, however so tiring and however so dirty, the girl did find enjoyment in hearing the little ducklings call for their mother, and in watching the lambs buck and play with one another.

Each animal truly must have been a pet, for all came up to the gate and behaved perfectly. Each wished to smell your hand, or wanting their head rubbed. Zinnia was very shy and had to be told to touch the little heads, before she would. With an unsteady hand she did as she was told, and found that these barn animals would not harm her. The sheep took her in with loving hearts and pranced happily about to entertain her, the ducks were not as light-hearted, yet they took to her as quickly as could have possibly been expected for a duck.

The horses especially fascinated Zinnia, with their large, brown, heart reading eyes, and snouts of velvet. They seemed to mirror exactly what was done to them. For instance, when Zinnia first approached them, she was full of nerves and her movements were abrupt and jerky, the horses did not react kindly to this. They began to back away, and grow uneasy at each advancement Zinnia made. Next, after June's advice on how to handle them, Zinnia went back to the stable of horses but this time moved slowly and with as much grace as her shaking hands would allow. Her hand met the nose of one of the horses. This one was gray, had kind eyes, and a gentle disposition.

"What is his name?" Zinnia asked with great curiosity.

"Well, actually it is a she, and her name is Nickel. She is my personal horse."

"She behaves perfectly."

"No, not always, but she *is* rather sweet. I have always loved her and I am sure you will too, in time."

"Oh, I already do. She is a complete darling! Would you mind telling me the names of the other horses?"

"Of course, the blonde one is Dove, another female, but the brown one, Clove, and the Appaloosa, Sisco, are both males."

"They are all so beautiful, but Sisco looks like no other I have ever seen. I wish he would come near the gate with the rest, and be friendly so I could pet him."

"Well, good luck with that, dear. Sisco is an ornery fellow who is alone by choice. I only wish he *would* be friendly so I could tame him down a bit, but he will have none of it."

"Oh, I see." Zinnia said thoughtfully.

Once the pair had finished feeding the horses their hay and grain, and were sure all of the other residents of the barn were happy, they began to put up the feed sacks and wheel barrel. June showed Zinnia where each and every thing belonged. She then said "Now, I will show you how to brush the horses. They are the only ones who need it every day. This is because if we do not untangle their manes, soon there will be knots of all kinds and the horses do not exactly volunteer to be brushed when it involves pain. Trust me, you do not want to be on the rear side of an enraged horse. It is altogether much easier if you simply give them a quick brushing every day."

They each took a brush, June opened the gate, but only wide enough to let Zinnia and herself slip through, and then with a light push, she shut it. You might have thought that the horses would be startled by or dreading the task at hand, but instead they seemed eager. June explained how the horses actually insisted upon being brushed.

"It makes my job much easier." she once laughingly admitted.

The magnificent creatures stood tall and proud, as they happily accepted their grooming. It was great fun to brush through their dusty manes until they were shining like silk, and pamper the horses until they lovingly rubbed against you. June took on Sisco, she got his mane fairly detangled, but it took grave effort and patience. Though, of course, by the end of the trying battle, Sisco was dubbed champion.

The barn work was then finished, so they went back towards the house. Zinnia chattered the whole way; she was full of new-found excitement and seemed to be bubbling over with joy. June found her constant babbling quite entertaining, for she was not use to watching the actions and hearing the thoughts of girlhood. Instead of going back inside, June lead the way to the garden.

"Morning or evening is the only time that I will ever water the garden, for the mid-day sun will evaporate all of our efforts to moisten the plants. Here is a water can, and the pump is near the back steps. Of course, you will have to pump the well by hand. I will water the carrots, spinach, and kale. You will water the beets, and the radishes. Come along with me, and I can show you were the rows are." June said as she went about collecting buckets for water. She seemed, to the girl, to never tire. There was much unexpected hard work that came with this way of life, but Zinnia was ready and willing for any hardships that might lay ahead of her.

# *Chapter XI*

# *June's Secret*

Within only a few months of living with June, Zinnia began to learn a great many things. It was difficult at first but June patiently taught the girl how to do all of the household chores, and Zinnia had even grown to enjoy them. Although she had always been nothing short from fine-looking, the young girl had become an absolute beauty. She was stronger and healthier, color warmed her ever-smiling face, and her heart was always light. She was growing more and more lovely with each coming day and had a simply charming personality.

One day, a look of disturbance struck Zinnia's face. She worriedly besought "June, what about your store? I had forgotten all about it. Shouldn't we go and look after it?"

"Oh, -er-yes. I suppose we should, but it really is no hurry."

"Why yes, it is. It is a great hurry indeed. What about all of those customers who are waiting? What about the dusting and cleaning that needs done?"

With that, Zinnia shot up, dropped the rag rug that she was braiding, and grabbed June's hand. She was pulling the dear woman towards the door.

"Wait darling, there is something you do not understand." sighed June.

"What could it be? I know all about the store, don't you remember telling me?"

"Yes, I do, but you see- the store has not been in business for quite a long time. All that I told you was true, but no one has come to my store for almost a year before you came-

"But why would it be open if there was no business? How could we have met if the door was not open?"

"Well, before you came to stay with me, I did not have much to occupy my time, after chores that is, so I went to my store and looked through the books."

"Oh, so I really just barged into your building and took up your time! Why didn't you stop me? How altogether awful! I am so sorry, June." cried Zinnia.

"No, no you mustn't be sorry. I loved your company. It is a blessing to this very moment! We should not discuss this any longer. You are getting upset, and my store is most definitely nothing to worry your pretty little head over. Try to forget it."

"Alright, June. If you wish me to forget it, I shall."

This news hit Zinnia with quite a shock, considering that June's store was the only reason for their encounter. Ah June, the woman who was responsible for such a drastic change in her life. She had nurtured and cared for the girl as if her own, and only wished her happiness. Therefore, Zinnia was forever thankful for this time-honored woman who showed her the beauty of life.

Time went on and soon Zinnia had forgot the sorrowful news about June's family store. There were many things to be done, for spring had come and was not shy in showing so. The birds were singing their love songs to one another, and the leaves upon each tree opened like hands praising the sun in all of its glory. The garden was fully planted and flourishing, just as most things do in May.

After all of the chores were done, June proposed that they take a stroll through the woods. Zinnia gladly accepted for she had not yet seen it. The two of them started down the sun speckled trail that lead into the thick line of green trees. Once they had entered the forest, everything suddenly became silent and still. The trees made a canopy over-head which protected them from the fiercely blowing wind. Although it was quiet, there still were plenty of ways to disturb the silence, for there were dead leaves scattered about the trail from the last season, as well as sticks just waiting to snap under the weight of a heavy unskilled foot. This foot, in fact, would be Zinnia's. She noticed how June could walk anywhere she pleased without making the slightest noise. This made Zinnia realize what a true racket she was making, so she quickly tried to adjust. It was much more difficult than she had imagined. It is nearly impossible to describe the show that this unskilled woodswoman was making. She was hopping all about trying her hardest to be quiet, although she very evidently was not succeeding.

Once, June looked back and saw what a struggle Zinnia was having, and could not help from laughing. Zinnia immediately heard this smothered chuckle, and said in attempts to defend herself "Now look here, June, I may not be as experienced as you but that is certainly no reason to laugh!"

"You are most certainly right; it is only that I have not seen anyone dance quite like that since I saw a drunken man jovially walking home!"

The girl tried to keep a straight face, but could not help from laughing after thinking of how she must look.

"You win. Now, will you please teach me the *right* way to walk through the woods?"

"Of course, dear. First, you are walking a little flat footed-

"I am?"

"Well, just a bit. You need to roll from the heel of your foot to your toe. Try to stay on the outside of your feet as well. Oh, and remember to bend your knees a bit as your foot hits the ground."

"My, but this sounds like more of a dance than what I was doing before!"

Although she felt silly, Zinnia tried her very hardest to do as June said. After a little diligent practice, her walking was no longer noisy, but instead, much softer and more cautious.

"This seems like an awful lot of unneeded work." Zinnia once thought to herself while she was struggling to do as she was told.

Soon, though, she got distracted from her odd task, for the forest around her was so enchantingly beautiful. There were delicate wildflowers within the woodlands, that waved their undaunted heads as if trying to catch the attention of the soon coming travelers. The creek that cut through the dense clump of trees was abundantly flowing and full of life. Beside it, Zinnia found the answer to why she was trying so hard to be silent, for there lay a white speckled fawn. She was curled up into a little ball, and was happily resting in the sun. Her eyes were like large black orbs, that looked observantly around enjoying each detail they hungerly consumed.

The delighted ladies stood there for no longer than a minute before the fawn's mother came into vision. The doe was not large, but she did seem to know exactly what she was doing, as she licked her little babe with the care only a mother could give. She did not stay long, though, before she sensed the tensely still figures that stood on the trail. With a turn of her keen ears and a snort that said nothing but "Come, now!", the doe and fawn were up and leaping above the over-grown masses of groundcover.

Once they had gone, Zinnia was full of delight and questions.

"June, was that the baby's mother? What made her know that we were here? Why did the baby not notice us? Where do you think they are going?"

"I am glad to hear that you care so much for the welfare of that small family. I know I always have had a soft spot for all animals. Now, one question at a time please, my dear. To answer the first, yes, I do suppose that that was the 'baby's mother', although it would be hard to tell for absolute sure. For question number two, because deer have a great many predators, they have been blessed with very alert senses. So therefore, she could have seen us move, smelled our scent, or heard us breathing. You may choose your pick, though I choose to believe it was a little of each. Lastly, there is no way to know where they are going, but I suspect that they will run until they feel that they are out of danger, then probably go back to doing the exact thing that they were doing before. For another thing, the 'mother deer' is called a doe, and the 'baby deer' are called fawns. Does that answer everything?"

"Why, yes. I believe it does." chuckled Zinnia "You sure do have a lot of spunk June, and I like it!"

"Well, thank you. I believe that is a painfully sufficient complement to an old, supposedly dignified, woman like myself!" grinned June "I think we might walk a little farther, but not for too much longer. If we were to walk the whole trail, it might take all day."

So, the pair did walk farther, a little farther in fact than was planned. At each corner there were specimens just waiting for them to see. One could never tire from the glory in which this forest beheld.

At one of these 'corners', there was a large river birch with a bird's nest resting upon one of the lower branches. The nest was most definitely not neat, it had small twigs and grasses poking out every-which-way. Zinnia pointed it out, and so they went to see if it had any occupants. It did indeed, there were two little mourning dove chicks. Their feathers looked matted, and their black beaks were knobby and cricked. They had to be one of the most hysterical sights that could be seen within the woods. They acted oddly and just sat there silently blinking their eyes, apparently waiting for their mother's return.

"That has to be the homeliest pair of birds I have ever seen." Zinnia giggled.

"Yes, but just think of what lovely birds they are sure to become. However, I have to agree with you, they are not exactly handsome to say the least."

They heard the mother coo to her young from a limb above, so they decided to leave the poor bewildered chicks alone. They then quickly realized that it had grown dark, and that it was high time they had left for home.

In the walk back through the woods, June told Zinnia the name of each spring wildflower they encountered, and Zinnia readily soaked up all of the knowledge that was showered upon her. The forest seemed even more lovely to the girl than it had before. This could have been because she now knew of the importance of the forest and of all the wonderful creatures and creations that prospered within its shielding leaves, or it might have been due to the glow that the orange sunset cast upon all of the newly found treasures and how the air filled her lungs with it's cool, sweet, dreamy aroma that only a spring night can give. No matter the reason, Zinnia's face beamed blissfully which resembled her completely over-flowing heart.

Once the pair got to the house, Zinnia fled to her notebook to write about her day. She had, just as she promised, written to her mother and father faithfully. Each letter she received from them talked of what marvelous things her father's money had bought. Some of these things might have tempted the girl in her past days, but now it all sounded like a bunch of good-for-nothing nonsense. Zinnia had grown to appreciate the once overlooked beauty in her life, and now knew that she was much happier for it.

# *Chapter XII*

# *Zinnia Meets Everit Cummings*

It was now the end of May, and things were going swimmingly. June and Zinnia got along perfectly. They never quarreled, yet they still were light-hearted enough to playfully banter every now and again. Zinnia knew all about the animals and loved to care for them, while June stuck to the cooking for Zinnia did not like *that* quite so well. As for Zinnia's apparent love for horses, she had found after a few experiments that the horses loved her back. She even had made headway with Sisco, he now was warming up to her and would even let her touch him if she feed him a sugar cube. June had shown the girl how to ride the horses, which became one of Zinnia's favorite uses of time.

On day, June suggested that they go for a ride and give some pastries as gifts to the not so nearby neighbors. Zinnia was happy to do it for she was, as always, anxious to ride. After June had the proper proportions for each family, they set off with three plates of delicious, warm, home-made desserts.

The first house they came to was at the end of the long road beside June's woods. There were lots of buildings on the property full of farming equipment or feed for their horses and cattle. The house itself was plain but large, it had a darling little flower patch and a vegetable garden the size of a field, though each were somehow perfectly maintained. As they were going down the lane June informed Zinnia that a Dutch family of eleven lived at the house, which made sense as to why they had multiples of everything. Once they pulled up to the house, a little girl with beautiful strawberry-blonde hair ran up to them.

"Hello." she said sweetly while displaying her most winning smile.

"Hello, my name is June. I am a neighbor of yours. Could you tell me where your parents might be?"

"Sure," she giggled "I am Lara. Mama is in the kitchen washin' strawberries and Papa is fixin' something with Ernest in the barn."

"Thank you very much, Lara, you have been of great help."

"Thank you, ma'am." With that she ran back to her sisters who were playing near a swing in the front yard.

"I think we will try the house first." June said laughingly, for little Lara had an unmistakable gift for making people smile.

They went up to the door, and after knocking heard a jolly "Come on in! The doors always open!" They did as the woman said, and found themselves in house full of laughing, playing children, each so obviously happy that they could not contain their joy any longer. Once they realized that someone was there for a visit, they hastily ran up and peered over each other's shoulders trying to get a glimpse at the new-comers. They behaved nearly perfectly, well at least as perfectly as little children could.

"Well, hello there. Sorry the house is such a mess, but with nine children-

"Oh, I understand completely, there is no need to be sorry. Children do have to play you know, and all of the sudden things accidentally get messy." June happily chirped.

"Precisely!" the woman exclaimed overjoyed, "Now, on what business were you brought here?"

"Oh, no business, no business at all. We only thought that since I made a few extra, you and your family might enjoy some pastries."

"Pastries!" yelled one of the rowdier boys.

"Yes, that is what the woman said isn't it? Now, please behave yourself and stay quiet until Mama is done visiting."

"Yes, Mama." said the remorseful boy obediently.

"Now," said the mother "what were you saying? Did I hear you say we?"

"Why, yes. This young woman that I brought with me is Zinnia Ellis. She has been staying with me to help with the chores. Well, we had better be going. We did not mean to intrude on you while you were working, we only meant to drop these off and be on our way." June said while setting the plate on the countertop.

"Well, thank you very much. It was nice to meet you Zinnia. What a pleasant surprise! I am sure that we all will enjoy these treats immensely. We will bring your plate back, and I am sure there will be something on it in return. It may be awhile though, we are always so busy, there truly never is a dull moment!"

"That is perfectly fine. I do not have any need for that plate, so you may keep it as long as you like. For now, I will be looking forward to your visit. Goodbye!"

"Goodbye, and thank you again!" called the good woman after they had left the room.

As they walked away, they heard the playful shrieks of the children once again. When they got back to their horses Zinnia said, "That woman has quite a lot to handle!"

"Yes, and she seems to be handling it well, if you ask me. Nine children and each equally obedient. Of course, they have a few slip ups every now and again, but that is to be expected."

"I agree, they were very respectful. I am already glad we came. Now, who may I ask, is next on the list?"

"Next, we are going to see a couple by the name of Washburn. It will not be as enjoyable of a visit as the last, but in order to be a kind neighbor sometimes you must endure those you are not so fond of."

"I see." said Zinnia with little understanding. She had never met any of her neighbors when she lived with her parents, excepting Elda, who they quickly tricked into being her family servant. Therefore, the girl knew quite little on the subject.

They rode about a mile before they reached a lonely gray house. It was right on the road and very stark. The horses acted timidly as they trotted up to the door, and Zinnia had to admit she felt the same. There were no gardens, barns, or bushes, they hadn't even a porch. The only thing that was brave enough to live in the presence of such a place, was one small maple tree, and even *it* was too afraid to show any sign of life.

June walked up to the door and located the old-fashioned knocker. With great audacity she rapped it.

"Yes?" came a meek voice from inside. Although, you could hardly call it a voice, it was much more like a screech.

"Hello, this is your neighbor, June McCafre. I have come to give you a few pastries that I have made."

"Come in, come in." said the voice as if drifting away.

June opened the door, and inside was an appalling sight. Every window had a curtain blocking out the sunlight, and the whole room appeared dreadfully hazy. Once they stepped inside, a small figure was detectable sitting on the sofa.

"Sit." she commanded in her ear-splitting tone.

June and Zinnia looked around, for there was hardly anywhere *to* sit. There was clutter everywhere and dust seemed to fill the air more than oxygen.

"No, we had better not." said June to Zinnia's relief "You see we have only come to drop the pastries off, and we really should be getting back to our horses. They have been acting a bit unusual."

"Oh, I see." said the woman with nearly no emotion.

"Who are you jabbering to!" yelled an impatient man from a different room.

"Oh, no one you'd care to see, only the neighbor!" the woman squealed back.

"You're full of hogwash, you old bat!" he nearly screamed back to her.

"Never mind him, he has always been rotten." stated the woman.

"Well, as I said we really should be going."

"Yes, bye."

With that, they left the horrid cave of a house, and re-entered into the bright sunshine of the afternoon.

"That is the most depressing room I have ever been in. I cannot even believe how ugly and disgusted those two-bickering old- er- people are with one another! She did not even say thank you!" Zinnia said as if her eyes and ears had been cheated their innocence.

"Yes, I know dear. I tried to warn you. They actually are not old; they are only in their forties, but they have allowed their unhappiness to be their eternal conqueror. Therefore, it is a life of downward depression for them. Maybe it was not a good idea to bring you here, but then, it is not good to live your life in the ignorance of how lovely it truly is. Seeing the misfortune of others can help us to be more thankful for what we *do* have, and to help those who need a steady hand."

"You are right, I suppose, as always. It is only that it is hard for me to see such hateful and disgraceful people."

"It is alright now, darling. Your life is shining as brightly as it ever has. Let this visit allow your light to shine brighter. We only have one more visit to make, and I am sure it will be a much more joyful occasion."

Zinnia just nodded and mounted her horse. They rode silently to the next home. As they neared their destination, Zinnia notice how June kept tucking stray hairs behind her ears. Once they arrived, June gracefully dismounted and carefully shook out her dusty skirt. Again, she smoothed her hair, then they proceeded to walk to the door. The house was of the same color of an evergreen tree. It was very neatly kept, but it somehow seemed to lack something.

June was acting in a way that was foreign to the girl. Zinnia had never seen her give a minute of care to her appearance, although she always was quite becoming. As June knocked on the door, she let out a nervous breath. Quickly her knock was answered, and in the doorway stood a tall older man. He was broad-shouldered, yet lean, with steel gray eyes that he could somehow make smile. His hair was of shining gray that was pushed upward where it met his forehead. To Zinnia his hair looked like an ocean's waves in moonlight.

"Why, what a pleasant surprise. How have you been, June?"

"I have been well. How are you Everit?"

"I have been as fine as ever. To what do I owe this wonderful visit?" Everit asked with a beam.

"Well, I made some cookies and I thought I would bring you some." June replied.

They stood there for an uncomfortable moment, then realized that they were staring at one another.

"Ah- thank you very much. I am sure they are delightful, just as the woman who made them."

"Oh," stammered June "no, I am not as good as that. My, I forgot to interduce you two. Everit, this is Zinnia Ellis, and Zinnia, this is Everit Cummings. Zinnia has been staying with me to help with the chores."

"Oh," the man said surprised. He acted as if he had never noticed Zinnia was there "how very nice it is to make your acquaintance."

"Thank you, and it is a pleasure to make yours, Mr. Cummings." Zinnia said, finally joining the conversation.

"Ah, won't you ladies come in?" Everit asked cordially.

To Zinnia's great surprise, June replied "Why yes, we would love to!"

And so, they entered the kind man's house. Inside, there was a comfortable seating area and a large bookshelf. Each piece of furniture was wooden, just as June's. Everything was kept very clean, minimal, and simple. Everit stepped to the side, and with an indicating sway of his arm said "Please, sit down." The women did as they were asked, and June sat the plate of pastries on the coffee table. Everit sat down as well, and began the conversation by saying "Well, it is certainly good to hear that you have someone to help you all year round. You have a mighty big farm. It would be a lot to handle for anyone."

"I manage, but thank you kindly for looking out for my well-being."

"Anytime, my dear."

June blushed bashfully, and then tried to smoothly change the subject "Yes, Zinnia here is a great help to me, she rapidly soaks up anything I teach her."

Zinnia spoke once again "Well, I would not say that. It is very hard to do all that you do in a day. It is all I can muster to fulfil the order of chores at hand. I simply do not understand how you do it, June."

"June here, is as strong as an ox, graceful as a swan, and delicate as a flower. She is a wonder to us all." Everit passionately protested.

At this complement, June's face no longer blushed, but now beamed. She tried to hush her giggling, but a few inevitably slipped out. Her flatterer heard this and said, "Oh, and do not forget, she also has a great sence of humor, a knock-dead gorgeous smile, and those wonderful wrinkles at the corner of each eye. Those tell you that she has had a life full of happiness, and a heart full of love."

Zinnia saw the struggle June was having to repress her embarrassment, so she tried to change the subject herself.

"So, Mr. Cummings, I see that you have quite a large bookshelf. Do you like to read?"

"Why, yes. I do."

"What is your preferred genre?"

"I mostly enjoy to forestry books. I love to learn about the birds and their habits, as well as the different types of trees. I pride myself in knowing what kind of tree it is just by looking at its leaf on the ground. As you can see, I do not have very many trees surrounding my house. I have planted the ones that *are* here, but I most definitely was not blessed with a forest. I also enjoy reading about different places to travel. Someday I hope to go sight-seeing, but I just have not found the time to pack up and leave.

"I did not know you liked forestry, so do I." breathed June "On my farm I have twenty-three untouched wooded acers. I know a bit about the trees on my property, but there are still hundreds that I know nothing of. Maybe sometime, if you are not too busy that is, you would be willing to come over and teach me a thing or two about the trees."

"Of course, I would love to!"

"Well, you may come over whenever your schedule allows. I am sure Zinnia and I will be there. We always are."

"Thank you immensely for your gracious invitation. I have been just itching to get into the woods, and gain some peace of mind. You have no clue as to what a savior you are to me."

"That sounds like a plan. Well, we had better be going, it is growing dusk."

"Yes, I suppose you must. Thank you for your visit, it was lovely. As always, you are more than welcome to stop in anytime you please. Your company means a lot to me." Everit said adoringly.

"As does yours, to me." June said with equal affection.

The women left the house, and walked to their horses. Once they got back to the road Zinnia said "Mr. Cummings seems to be a very nice fellow."

"Why, yes. He is quite a gentleman." June replied wistfully.

She seemed to be preoccupied, so Zinnia kept her mouth shut for the rest of the ride home. It was not hard, for the world around them had changed into what seemed to be a charming land from a fairytale. In the west, the sky was blazing with the same fiery pink as an old-fashioned rose, but in the center of this dome was the never-ending depth of serene blue. The night was so lovely that the line between real life and a dream was blurred, allowing all to join together to form one alluring mass of beauty. The horses had to nearly drive themselves home, for their masters were both too enchanted to make sense of anything. Once they arrived to the house in the woods, they dismounted and stabled their horses. They walked down the hill and into the house, where they finally began to talk.

"This was a very peculiar night. I was so calm, I should say I could have nearly slide off Dove, fallen asleep on the road, and never made a peep!"

"Yes, it was quite serene. Thank you for coming along with me to deliver those pastries. It was very nice to have your company."

"Thank you for taking me with you. I enjoyed it. I had better write my mother her letter and be off to bed. Good night, June." Zinnia said as she drowsily crept up the stairway.

"Good night, dear. Have sweet dreams." June called softly after her.

A little while later June herself slid into bed, but sleep would not come. She tossed and turned, trying desperately to get comfortable in hopes that would solve her sleeplessness. It did not, for her mind was restless and could not be quieted.

# *Chapter XIII*

# *Peter Wells Unexpectedly Arrives*

The next morning, Zinnia awoke earlier than usual. After going down stairs and seeing that June was not occupying the kitchen, Zinnia decided to look out the window. There, she saw the sun barely peeking out from above the horizon line. She sat down, not knowing what to do with herself, for June had always awoken much earlier than she ever had. After thinking the situation over, Zinnia murmured to herself "I suppose I could go out and finish the morning chores. Yes, I think that would be best, and it *would* make June quite proud of me."

It was then decided, so out into the brisk morning air Zinnia went. She did her chores merrily, first feeding the chickens, then the rest of the animals that were up in the barn. The little fleecy lambs leaped about jovially, and the ducks squawked and beat their wings. Zinnia fed the horses last in hopes that she would have plenty of time to spoil them, and not be hurried with the thought of unfinished chores.

They all seemed to be in an abnormally charming demeanor, even Sisco, who seemed to pride himself in being particularly vile. Zinnia walked straight up to the steel gate that enclosed these gorgeous creatures, opened it, and stepped inside the stable, just as she had now for months. Usually, three of the four horses came right up to her and greedily nosed her pockets for their small cube of sugar, Sisco of course, was the one who deliberately stayed behind, so that *you* had to come to *him*. On this day though, he came to her with the rest of the group. Zinnia was completely overjoyed.

After taking in this new-found trust that Sisco had so evidently shown towards her, Zinnia decided to test the waters and see just *how* much he trusted her. First, she stroked his mane, just as she always did. Then his snout, which she had attempted once or twice before but failed. This time, though, she was conqueror, for Sisco did not only allow this affection, but seemed to enjoy it. Seeing this detestable horse's change, gave Zinnia a sudden streak of courage which seemed to come out of nowhere. Before she knew it, Zinnia mounted the horse, and to her surprise, he did not buck or show a waiver of discontent. He stood there, looking as if he were only waiting for her signal, and so she gave it. With a swift click of her tongue, Sisco was off. He ran like a bolt straight through the pasture, racing faster and faster. Zinnia was nearly thrown off, and being senseless enough to put nothing on him but a bridal, did not help matters any.

She was helplessly flying through the wind on the back of an unbroke, untrained animal. Having no other power, all she could do was shriek "Stop!" To her surprise the horse actually did what she said, although she nearly got thrown headlong over him. Luckily, she held fast to Sisco's mane, resulting in no serious injuries, she was only a little shaken up. For several minutes Zinnia sat on the motionless horse, feeling utterly stupefied. Once she had taken a few shaky breaths and regained her composure, she patted Sisco and realized the importance of his sudden obedience. Together the pair went back to the barn, but unlike ever before, they both held full trust in one another.

Once they arrived, Zinnia dismounted. She felt entirely rapturous. Her cheeks were blazing, and her eyes shown with a new brightness. Each step she took was proud, mirthful, and full of excitement. She was a perfect image of girlhood. She stepped out from behind the gate, and then looked back at the horses through the metal bars. Sisco was right there, standing in front of her with his large eyes looking with admiration down into hers. Zinnia reach out and touched his shining nose once again.

She then breathed "You are a true mystery," but before she could finish, a voice called out "Well upon my word, you can touch em'! And he appears to be a likin' it, too!"

Zinnia took a sharp breath in, for this voice was unknown to her, and she had not known that she was not alone. She quickly spun her head in the direction of the voice, and there standing in the barn path was a young man.

"You must be getting soft in your old age, Sisco!" he chuckled as if it were some kind of worthy joke.

"How do you know his name!" gasped Zinnia.

"Well, he is *my* horse. Who are you anyhow?"

"Excuse me sir, but I do not believe I know exactly who *you* are either. Seeing that I live here, and that *you* barged in on *me*, it seems only fitting that you should be the one answering that question." Zinnia with growing angrier towards this unknown man.

"Live here! Now wait just a dadgum minute, no girl lives here, only an old lady!"

"How dare you! Tell me who you are before I go get something that will make you!"

"Alright, alright," the man said lifting his hands up to show he was no threat, "I am Peter Wells. There, now your turn."

"No, first tell me what it is you are doing here, Peter Wells." Zinnia commanded unconvinced.

"I am here to visit my aunt. I stay here every summer to help her. Now will you tell me who *you* are?" he asked coaxingly.

"If this woman is your aunt, then tell me her name." Zinnia said with little trust.

"Her name is June McCafre. Satisfied?" he said humorously.

Zinnia had to admit she was finding his story somewhat believable.

"Now, if you please, will you tell me what your name is?" he asked determinedly.

"My name," she hesitated, "is Zinnia Ellis."

"Alright, now your turn, what is it that has brought *you* here." he persisted.

"I met June at her store, and she told me she would like help around the house, so here I am."

"See, now was that so bad?" Peter questioned with a charming smile.

Zinnia had to admit that he was not exactly an unsightly fellow. His hair was golden brown, just the color of a dried tulip tree leaf, yet his eyes were of the most fascinating blue and seemed to read and understand all of your emotions. He was, in fact, quite a handsome and interesting young man. Although in this instance, she was not inclined to say any such thing that could perhaps show weakness.

Peter continued "I went to the door and knocked, but no one answered, so I figured Aunt June was up here feeding the livestock. Instead, I found you."

"Well, if what you say is true, then I am very sorry for my rudeness." Zinnia said shortly.

"Well, I am sorry for startling you like I did." Peter said graciously.

This made Zinnia smile, and she began to trust him.

"So, Zinnia, how *did* you get Sisco to warm up to you, anyhow?"

"I just kept attempting to show him affection and I suppose he finally excepted it. But I do not wish to talk of this at present, so why don't we go to the house and see how your story sums up?"

"Yes, I would love to go see Aunt June, if you would escort me-

"Of course."

Off the two went, walking down the dewy hill. After arriving at the house, Zinnia called through the door to June, who had now awoken and had breakfast served.

"June, there is a young man here that claims he knows you. He says his name is Peter Wells."

Zinnia hardly finished her sentence before an excited cry sounded from the kitchen.

"Oh, Peter! Oh, Peter!" she ran to the door, "My, look at how you've grown."

"Hello, Aunt June it is great to see y-

He also never finished his sentence, for he was entrapped in a crushing hug.

"Oh Peter, I am so sorry! I forgot about your coming, I have been so busy! I see you have already met Zinnia; she has been staying with me."

"Yes, that is what she told me. It seems you have a good protector. She nearly kicked me off of the property!" he laughed.

"Oh," said the woman appearing to misunderstand.

"No, do not think anything bad of Zinnia, it was my fault. I frightened her, for she did not know me or of my coming. It was a perfectly understandable mistake."

Zinnia blushed bashfully, then said with great sorrow "I truly am sorry, Peter. I did not think you were being honest, and I admit I was too protective,"

"As I said, it is perfectly understandable. Think nothing of it."

"Yes, dear," piped in June "it is quite alright. I am glad to know you are watching out for me."

Zinnia laughed, then said "Well, I am glad to know I am, too. Though, if we were being truthful June, you have looked out for me much more than I ever have for you."

Now it was June's turn to blush. She quickly exclaimed "Well, I will not hear anymore about it. Why don't you two quit standing around outside, and come in and have some breakfast."

They did what they were told, and obediently went in and stood by the wooden table. The reason why they would not sit, was because there were only two chairs and they did not know who should sit and who should not. June saw this, and somehow produced a chair from the corner. She sat it on one of the sides near another chair. Zinnia went to the other side where the lone chair stood, but before she could sit June said "Now wait just a minute, you should sit on the same side as Peter. I would like to see you both at the same time." she finished with a smile.

Zinnia did as June wished, but winced with embarrassment all the while. Peter, on the other hand, appeared to be as undisturbed as usual. After saying grace, they began their hardy meal.

"I am so happy to have you here." June declared. "So, how are your parents?"

"They are quite well. Mother is very anxious for warmer weather, and father is as grand as ever. He is going on a trip to Elkhart for some parts, you know he has been trying to fix something up to give mother. Well anyhow, whatever it is, he is all tickled about it."

"Why, Elkhart is where Zinnia's parents are traveling. Maybe your father will run into them." joked June.

"Oh, you are from Elkhart?" Peter asked Zinnia.

"No, actually my parents are just now moving there. I decided to stay here and help June." answered the girl.

"How long are you staying here?" he again comfortably questioned.

"Well, I am not exactly sure. How long will you be staying?"

"Oh, I normally stay till' August." he said nonchalantly. "I love this table Aunt June. Did Mr. Cummings make it for you?"

"Ah- yes." she cautiously admitted.

Zinnia looked over at June in complete astonishment. “Why June, you never told me that! Did he make any of your other furniture?”

“Yes, he did. In fact, he made nearly all of it.” she answered meekly.

“Why, I’ll be danged! That is quite a lot of carving to be done by just one man!” Peter interjected.

“Yes, it would take quite a lot of *loving care*.” Zinnia hinted ruthlessly.

“You two have some very deranged notions.” June stammered, trying to take the spotlight off of herself.

The talk went on, and soon they had learned quite a great deal about one another. After breakfast was finish and cleaned up, June asked Zinnia and Peter to go out and water her flower garden. This was quite a large task, for there were row after row of voluminous flowers who each needed a hefty drink. Peter led the way to the pump and started to fill the buckets with water. Zinnia could only take but one pail at a time, while Peter could carry two large buckets with ease. She realized this, and so commented “You sure can carry a lot of water. It is a great help to have you with me.”

“As are you to me, for each pail you bring makes one less for me.” he laughed jovially.

“So, what do you do when you are not helping June?” Zinnia asked.

"Oh, sometimes I help in the field and sometimes I work in my father's store."

"What does your father sell?"

"Peaches-

"Really? I love peaches, but there seems to be few grown here locally."

"Well, we've got peaches a mile high. I almost am sick of em' by the end of the season, yet by the next year my mouth's watering for em'. Hey, weren't you going to tell me how you got Sisco all lovey over you? I have been trying to crack that nut for years!"

"Oh, yes!" Zinnia laughed "I suppose he just got use to me. I see him every day, and each time I do I give him a sugar cube in hopes to pet him."

"So, you're turning him into a butterball are ya?"

"Yes, I suppose." giggled the girl.

"Oh, I forgot to tell June, but today I rode him! He was faster than anything, and I almost fell off, but he was obedient and-

"What! You rode him! You must be crazy! He could have easily hurt you, and I could not live with myself if *my* horse hurt *you*!"

"But, he didn't. Do remember that fact."

"Yes, I suppose you are right." sighed the young man. "Whenever we get done with this job let's go see how our old butterball is doing."

"That sounds like a fine idea." declared Zinnia.

# *Chapter XIV*

# *An Evening Ride*

After Peter and Zinnia told June that they were going to the barn, the pair carried out their plan. Once they got to the barn, Zinnia asked "How did you get Sisco, Peter?"

"He was a colt from one of June's neighbors, and when I was a boy she bought him for me as a gift. He was just as wild then, but of course we supposed he would grow out of it. Now, as I am sure you know, he did not."

"Yes, he wasn't exactly a sweetheart." commented Zinnia.

After talking for a while, Peter decided he was going to attempt to ride Sisco. He may have wanted to see if his horse had really changed, or perhaps he just wanted to show off for the altogether captivating and lovely girl whom he had just met. No matter the reason, he proudly mounted the horse, though he was not on him for long, for Sisco reared up and off tumbled Peter. Zinnia rushed to his side and worried over him just as most woman would do, although there was still a part of her that was proud of how Sisco trusted her only.

Zinnia held out her hand as to help Peter up. The young man took it, and with his other he wiped the dust from his britches.

"Well, that did not work out how I planned." Peter sighed thoughtfully.

"That is quite alright Peter, I am sure he will get use to you soon." Zinnia said, all the while trying to hide the mischievous smirk that had creeped upon her face. Though her efforts were in vain, for Peter read her emotions and almost immediately commented on them.

"Are you laughing at me? Come now, don't try to hide it!" he laughed light-heartedly.

That was one of the many lovable traits about him, he never was stern or cross, and when he made a mistake he simply laughed without showing the slightest bit of embarrassment.

Zinnia now realized something she hadn't before, Peter was, in fact, still holding her hand. She took an uneasy breath in as she looked down at their hands clasped together. Peter saw this and let go, to Zinnia relief yet somehow disappointment.

Peter was first to change the subject "Do you have a nickname?"

Zinnia was taken by surprise "Ah- no. I was never given one."

"Well, then I will give you one. It shall be Flower. Of course, there is the obvious reason, being Zinnia is a type of flower, but then also, because you are just as beautiful as one."

Zinnia was blushing crimson, and could only bring herself to say "I like that name."

They stood there for a minute just looking at one another. To Peter, Zinnia truly was lovelier than any flower ever attempted to be. Her hair laid in long brown curls that ran down her back, it was pulled neatly away from her radiant face, although, a few stray untamed curls still persisted to frame her temples. Then after realizing that he was not being courteous, he turned away.

"We really should be getting back to June." murmured Zinnia.

"As you wish, Flower" answered Peter with his handsome eyes shining.

A wide smile stretched across Zinnia's face as the two of them walked down the hillside. Before they could reach the house, they met June in the driveway.

"Why, hello my dears. I was just going up to check on you two."

"I am sorry we kept you waiting, but Flower and I were looking at Sisco. She has him all warmed up to her."

June looked at Zinnia quizzically, and found the girl to be almost unearthly with beauty. Her face shone like a perfect angel, and it seemed no more excitement nor happiness could possibly be attained. Then looking at her beloved nephew, she found him too to be completely entranced.

"Flower?" questioned June.

"Yes," chuckled Peter, seeing the misunderstanding in his aunt's face. Then looking at Zinnia he softly spoke, "that is the nickname I gave Zinnia."

Nothing, in June's mind, could have caused this except for one simple thing, love. At first the idea was a little overwhelming to the dear old woman, but after carefully taking in the facts she decided it would be quite a lovely thing after all. She cared for both of them as if they were her own, and could not name anyone with a more honest heart than either of them.

After collecting herself, June grinned at the youthful faces in front of her and thought of how wonderful it truly was to be in love.

"I was wondering if you two would enjoy going on a ride this evening?"

"Oh, could we?" asked Zinnia excitedly.

"I know I would love to go." answered Peter "Flower could probably ride Sisco if she coaxed him." joked Peter.

"What? Ride Sisco? That is impossible."

"That's what I thought Aunt June, but Flower has proved that it most definitely is not. She has already ridden him and-

"Please tell me you are only kidding." Their faces showed that they were not. "Zinnia, you could have been seriously injured and I could not bear the thought of you getting hurt while in my care! I love you too much for that!

Just tell me what I would have told your parents!" fumed June.

"I'm sorry June; something just came over me and I could not control it. It was immature and thoughtless of me. Even after considering all of these things though, I did not get hurt. I am as well as ever, and we have a horse that is one step closer to being tamed. I promise from here forward that I will be less reckless, and that I will think of the consequences before I take action. Oh, please forgive me, June."

This apology was sufficient enough to calm June's rapidly climbing nerves.

"It is quite alright, darling. I know how sometimes logical decisions do not take place in our minds; it has happened to me many a time before. You are forgiven. Let us forget this whole ordeal."

They all walked to the little slate colored house. Since it had grown to be early evening, and none of them were hungry for their breakfast was enough to keep them full all day, they decided to put on a change of clothes for their ride. June had on a particularly cunning blue dress, it was light in color, though the fabric had many deeply colored bouquets scattered about it. This was a bit of an odd occurrence considering it was only a horse ride down a dusty dirt road. She also had her hair pinned up on the crown of her head. A waterfall of waves fell from the messy bun in the most delicate way. Zinnia also had on a charming dress, it was colored in dusty rose with little pleats all around the waist and wide flowing sleeves which fell around her wrists. Her hair was braided in a long rope that reached the small of her back. Still the small curls hung framing her face, which Peter so evidently adored. Peter himself was dressed in handsome attire. His riding pants were of a light caramel color, he had on shining black boots that reached his knees, and he wore a white tunic with soft billowy sleeves.

Since Peter was a courteous man and he had finished dressing before the others, he went to the barn on the hill and saddled the horses. Then taking them by the reins, he led Nickle, Dove, and Clove to their post near the porch. After a moment of waiting, two dashing women exited the door. Peter stood there in awe.

“I had no clue I was to dress so nicely for this ride. Are we going somewhere special?” he questioned.

“No, nowhere special. We just thought it would be fitting to put on lovely dresses for a lovely evening.” This statement of June’s save Zinnia’s case as well as her own, for both of them very well knew that they had never dressed so elegantly in times past.

“We had better get going.” June continued “Oh, but I forgot something in the house. You two can ride to the end of the lane, and I will catch up.”

With that June swiftly reentered the house, while Zinnia and Peter were left standing on the porch looking after her. Zinnia sweetly turned to Peter and smiled. In response, he bowed as if she were his queen and then extended his arm for her to take. Zinnia did exactly as Peter hoped and took it. They walked to their horses, each feeling more anxious with every step. Once they arrived, Peter helped his "Flower" to her saddle, and then mounted his own horse. Together they set the horses gently trotting, though they did not stay that way for long. Soon the two of them were off and racing, stirring dust up all the way. They were neck and neck, and Peter's instinct wanted nothing more but to win the race, but his heart told him otherwise. The gentleman pulled on his reins the slightest bit, his horse slowed, and Zinnia won the race.

"I could have sworn you were going to beat me!" Zinnia exclaimed breathlessly.

"You wouldn't be the only one! That was a tough match, you are a fantastic rider. How long have you been racing?"

"This is my first time." caroled Zinnia joyously.

"Well, you are pretty darn good, Flower, for a first timer." Peter declared with a now even happier heart.

Seeing Zinnia so altogether radiant with delight sent the poor lad over the moon for her. He was earnestly interested in her every movement, and had an uncontrollable urge to worship the ground she stood upon. For now, though, all he could do was smile.

"Well, now we must wait for June." the blissful girl stated in a sing-song sort of way.

It was, in fact not so long of a wait, for June sped up the drive at such a speed that she could have easily beaten Peter and Zinnia both. They then set off as one uncommonly fine-looking group. They rode for around fifteen minutes before they came to Everit Cummings's house, there June commenced to fixing her hair and dusting off her skirt just as before. Then she said "I brought a little dessert for Everit, so I am just going to drop it off. He may not be home or he may want to visit, so don't wait up for me. Let us meet back at my place around eight-thirty."

"That sounds just fine Aunt June."

"Yes, we will see you later. Have a nice time." added Zinnia.

"You as well." June answered succinctly.

And so, the threesome split.

"Where do we intend to go?" questioned Zinnia curiously.

"Well, I know of a very lovely road, it has old dilapidated barns, rows of trees, and young quail at one of the fence posts-

"Oh, that *does* sound lovely. Let's go!"

"Alright, but it is quite a few miles away, are you sure you want to go tonight?"

"If you think we can make it back in time, then we should go. I have no doubt in your words any longer."

"That is quite a relief." laughed Peter in his usual jocular way.

# *Chapter XV*

# *June's Dream Materializes*

After June had arrived at Everit's house, she knocked on the door, although before she could finish her knock, it was answered.

"Why, hello Everit. I am sorry to bother you this evening, but I made some cookies for you -er- I mean I made a few extra cookies and I was wondering if you would like some."

"You are no bother June, I love having you here, and I am sure your cookies are simply too wonderful to refuse. Won't you come in?"

"Yes, of course." June affectionately agreed.

"Sit down. I have some tea in the kitchen that we can drink. I will go get it."

"Alright, thank you kindly." June genially replied.

It took Everit quite a while to come back with the tea, and when he did, he seemed horribly nervous.

"Thank you, Everit." repeated June.

"No, thank you June. Your company means everything to me." stated the gentleman. Then he paused "It is such a lovely evening; would you like to sit beneath one of my trees and watch the sunset?"

"I would love to. It truly would be a pity to let the beauty of the night go unnoticed." stated June blushing all the while.

Everit lead the way to a monstrous pine tree that sat beside the house. There he brushed away all of the pine cones and needles that could possibly stain June's dress.

"How thoughtful of you. That is quite a lot of work though, you need not go to all of the effort."

"Oh yes, I do! How could I possibly allow the most beautiful creature on earth to dirty her dress for my desire of being outdoors?"

"You must be delirious Everit! I am no where near even fine-looking, and if you would be so kind as to remember, I *also* wished to come out of doors."

"June, you are the most wonderful person I have ever met. You are perfectly balanced in all ways. I dare say, if you met the devil himself, you could look him straight in the eye and not show a mite of fear, you could turn down any offer he made, and all the while look just like a delicate angel of the Lord."

"Oh, you are completely wrong!" interjected June feverishly.

"No, indeed I am not, and I am not finished with setting you straight on what is true. Now, ever since I have met you, you have greatly enlivened my life and recreated my perspective. I always am distinctly more amiable when I am around you, for your wonderful spirit has forced me to become a much more improved and rightous man. I have been acting like an ignorant old fool, for I have been altogether too terrified to state the simplest fact; the fact that my life has revolved around since the day we met. June, I love you. I always have, and I always will. I am asking you to marry me, June, but I understand if you reject me, for I am only a blundering old fool in love."

"Oh, Everit, I accept! I have loved you always!"

June was to overjoyed to say anything more. She could not, even if she had tried, for Everit had enwrapped her in a zealous yet tender kiss. As he did so, he slipped a simple but elegant ring on her finger. June payed little attention to the valuable token of love that was now in her possession, instead her eyes were steadily set upon the man to whom her heart now ardently belonged.

The evening had grown into the most magnificent of settings. Zinnia rode happily beside Peter as they turned back towards the direction in which they had come, passing Everit's house and their own house once again. They turned down a road that followed a copiously flowing river. The view was breathtaking. Each tree appeared to be dark and full of unknown treasures, the grass was lighted with the orange sunset, and the animals ran carelessly about.

"It is a truly lovely night." Zinnia said as she wistfully looked about her.

Peter had not noticed, for he was only looking at her. "Yes, lovely..." he trailed off.

They soon came to a path that lead into a forest towards the river. They stopped their horses, and Zinnia looked longingly into the mass of trees.

“I wonder who owns these woods.”

“It is a nature preserve, no one owns it. I have walked through it many times before.”

“Couldn’t we walk it now?” pleaded Zinnia “I would enjoy it so very much.”

Peter could not deny his Flower anything that could possibly bring her happiness, so he agreed. Zinnia hopped down from her horse, and tied it to a nearby tree. Peter did the same, but he was hardly finished before Zinnia pulled him away eagerly. They wandered down the quaint trail and experience every blessing that Mother Nature held for them. There were dutchman breeches and bleeding hearts in full bloom, and too many yellow, white, and purple, violets to count. The squirrels gave an acrobatic show of agility in the treetops, and the robins gave a sonorous concert. The path did eventually lead to the river which swiftly flowed, as usual for that time of year. The pair found two rocks that lined the water and sat silently upon them for a time, listening to all of the sounds, and watching the blue herons wade in the shallowest part of the water. Peter looked over at the lovely young lady who was resting near him.

“Flower,” Peter said deep in thought. To her name, Zinnia spun her head around. Then Peter continued looking straight into her bewildered eyes “never has that name better fit you.”

Zinnia blushed and looked down. Then after meeting Peter's adoring eyes once again, she said "You are quite a flatterer, aren't you Peter Wells?"

"It comes easily when you have such a beautiful piece of poetry sitting right in front of you."

Just then the winds picked up, fiercely howling and thrashing their teeth. The sky turned from orange to gray in a heartbeat.

"Flower, we have to get out of here! A storm is coming!" yelled Peter trying to compensate for the crashing of the waves that now fled around them. He grabbed her hand and lead her back to the ground. He never let go, even as they ran with all of their might. Suddenly, a down pour of rain fell from the appalling sky. It drenched the two of them until Zinnia nearly cried with fear. They kept running, but Zinnia started to fall behind. Her hand slipped from Peters' and she quickly yelled "Peter! Help, I'm stuck!" The young man turned around, but before he could do anything for his beloved Flower, a strike of lightning shook the ground around him. Then everything went black.

Once he awoke, he found himself lying beneath a charred black tree, with water filling in around him. His arm had blood flowing in a steady stream, his head was bruised from the impact of his fall, and both of his legs were trapped under the heavy tree. Immediately he looked for Zinnia, but what he found made him feel much worse, for the girl was not making any movement and she laid in a deep, murky, puddle of mud. Peter tried to free himself from beneath the fallen tree. He pushed as hard as he could against it, but the tree would not budge. Every strenuous attempt he made was in vain, for still the tree was immoveable. He decided to take a different approach, he began clawing with his fingernails into the sinking mud and pulling himself forward. This technique surprisingly worked, after realizing that he was making headway, Peter pulled himself through the muck with all of the force he could muster. Finally, his legs were free. He could not feel them nor stand on them for they were completely numb. He had to nearly drag himself to Zinnia. All the while, the rain relentlessly fell and thunder continually resounded with such a clash that is made your soul shiver.

Once he came within reach of Zinnia, he saw her dreadfully pale face, there seemed to be no life within it. His shaking hand touched her throat, and to his reluctance, her heart was still slowly beating. After seeing someone he cared so much for look terribly close to the immoral jaws of death, Peter found the sudden strength to lift himself to his feet. Soon the girl was in his arms, and he was running fearlessly through the daunting forest. He could hardly look at Zinnia, for the sight of her powerless head draped over his forearm and her white hands that limply laid upon her breast, wrenched the boy's heart until tears swiftly streaked down his soiled face.

Finally, Peter reached the rearing horses. He took his own, and with Zinnia in his arms, rapidly took off. After twenty minutes of reckless riding, Peter reached his familiar summer home. To his relief, a light came from within the house. He delivered Zinnia to the front porch, before June and a large man quickly assisted him.

"My dear boy! Hurry you must come in!" cried June as she acted as Peter's crutch.

The man quickly caught Zinnia from Peter's slipping arms, and took her into the shelter of the house.

"You are bleeding all over! You must sit down! Peter, please!"

"No, I am fine. Will she be alright?" Peter asked delirious with worry.

But before he could hear his answer, the overwhelming excitement, the gnawing torment of trouble, and the vile pain that had grown in his arm, all became to much for the lad. And so, again, everything went black.

# Chapter XVI

## The Unconscious Awaken

Peter awoke later that night, and found himself lying on a bed in a dark room. At first, he remembered nothing, then very shortly everything flew back to his memory. Immediately, he sat up in the bed, but before his feet could reach the floor, a horrid pain shot through his arm. Then his head began to spin at such a speed that it hurt to even open an eye. Completely disgusted with his languor, Peter decide to resort to yelling.

"Aunt June! Aunt June!"

The door flew open, and in rushed the light and the woman.

"What is it, Peter! Are you alright?" she asked worriedly.

"Where is Flower? Is she all right?" Peter repeated breathlessly.

"You should not worry about her now, Peter. You have yourself to think of."

"Aunt June," he said sternly "is she alright!"

"Yes, my boy. She will be fine."

"Has the doctor seen her yet? What did he say?" the young man ruthlessly besought.

"Yes, the doctor came about an hour ago. He saw you both. Zinnia is running a high fever but we are sure she will be over it in a few days. You, on the other hand-

"Forget about me. Is she still unconscious?" he asked urgently.

"Peter-

"Please answer the question!"

"Yes, she still is, but I am sure she will wake up soon, just as you have. Now Peter, about you-

"Someone should be with her, looking after her! Don't waste your time on me! Go to her!"

"Everit is in the other room with the girl right now! There is nothing to worry about! Now, you listen to me and you listen well, if you wish to see Zinnia as soon as possible, then lay back down and work on feeling better yourself.

"You had an in lodged piece of rock in your left arm that the doctor had to operate on, your right arm is broken, both of your legs are thoroughly bruised from the waist down, you have a mild concussion, and a dreadfully high fever. Zinnia will be fine; you are much worse off and so I suggest you stop worrying over her!"

Peter laid back among his pillows, and took a deep sigh of relief. Then after hearing his own situation, he began to think.

"Peter, how are *you* feeling?"

“I feel fine.” Peter winced, apparently trying his hardest to sound believable. June was not so easily convinced.

“Is there anything I can do for you, darling?”

“No, but thank you Aunt June.”

“Then I will let you be so you can get some rest.” With that, June softly crept from the room.

Across the hall she went to go check on Zinnia. Inside the room she found the girl still lying there with her frail hands clasped over her breast. Everit sat in a chair nearby, keeping close watch on the unconscious girl.

“Is she doing any better?” June anxiously questioned.

“Well, I suppose she will awake soon. She has been tossing and turning all about the bed, and mumbling something that I can’t quite understand. I believe she will soon come to.” the kind man reported gently, in attempts to soothe his soon-to-be bride.

“You must be terribly tired. I will go make us some coffee. Call for me if she awakens.”

“I will, my love.”

June could not help but smile at this, for in all of the excitement she had almost forgotten that she now had a loyal man who loved her with all of his heart. She new that she felt the same towards him. Her spirits lifted as she entered the kitchen and started the process of grinding coffee beans. Just as she got the boiling pot of black energizer off of the burner, she heard a call.

"June..." came Everit's uncertain voice.

The woman dropped what she was doing and hurried to the bedroom. There she found Zinnia rolling her head back and forth on her pillow. Her eyes were closed and she was groaning in agony. Then her eyes opened, but only into tiny slits. She started to shiver.

"June?" she murmured piteously.

"Yes, my love. I am right here." June then bent down and started stroking the girls blazing hot forehead. Perspiration was beading in groups on her temples, and now her face was glowing a brilliant red. June went on trying to assist the girl in any way she could. She bathed Zinnia's face with wet cloths, and pulled the blankets away and then back over her continuously, trying to help the girl through her ever-changing temperature swings.

Peter slept the rest of the night through and was little to no problem, so June and Everit sat watching over Zinnia as she battled her fever.

"I am so sorry that you have to be stuck here while all of this is going on." sighed June.

"You are here, and so there is no other place I would rather be." Everit affectionately replied.

He wrapped his arm around June and pulled her close. June leaned her head on his broad shoulder, and there she fell asleep. Everit carried her down the stairs and into her bed, were he tucked her in and kissed her goodnight. Then back to his post he went, determinately waiting and watching for any subtle changes in Zinnia's health. At about seven in the morning, he got what he had prayed so strenuously for. The girl awoke.

"Where am I?" she muttered.

"You are back in your room, at June's house. I will go get her."

"Wait! Where is Peter? Is he alright?"

"Let me go get June. She can explain things better than I." Then Everit hurried from the room.

He knocked on June's door saying "Darling, I am sorry to wake you, but Zinnia's fever has broken and she wants you."

Instantly the door flew open, and June went jogging up the stairs. Once she came to Zinnia's room, she tried to settle herself, in hopes to not startle the girl with any unneeded excitement.

She entered the room "I am here, dear."

"Oh June, I am so sorry we were so far away! It was all my fault! How is Peter?"

"He has been pretty severely hurt, but he acts as if he has no pain whatsoever. He will be well soon. For now he is sleeping, but do not worry yourself over him for he is well enough himself to worry over you. He awoke at around midnight and his every question was considering you."

"Oh, he is too sweet. Even in all of his pain he is selfless enough to think of others-

"No, dear. Not others, you. He is a fine gentleman. I am very proud of him. Now, how are you feeling?"

"I am feeling much better. Couldn't I get up to see him?"

"I think you better rest for a few more hours, just to play it safe. I could not endure anymore disaster for one night."

"Yes, June." Zinnia replied obediently.

And so, Zinnia slept until about noon. When she aroused, she heard the sound of frying and boiling coming from the kitchen. After realizing that June and Everit would be too busy to notice, the girl noiselessly slipped from her bed and crept across the hall to where she expected Peter to be resting. Her intuition was correct, for in the bed Peter lay, looking up at the ceiling and twiddling his thumbs. He glanced over at the door when he heard it creak.

"Flower-

"Oh Peter," Zinnia said rushing to his side "I am so sorry! This is all my fault!"

"No, it most definitely is not! It is all mine! How could I do this to you! I am such a fool!"

"Peter, stop this talk at once! It is not wise for us to disagree, especially in your condition."

"Well, do you need anything?"

"Peter! You are the one who needs looked after! Are you comfortable? Can I get you anything?"

"I am fine, thank you Flower."

Zinnia looked closer at her gallant knight, and saw all of his horrid wounds.

"Oh my, what is the matter with your arms! Can you move them?"

"Aunt June says that ol' Doc had to operate on one of them and that the other one is broken." He said non-chalantly.

"And your head! It is all bandaged up! What happened?"

"Aw, it's only a concussion."

"You are simply incredible! I do not understand how you could possibly act so strong; you amaze me!"

Peter was beaming at this remark, when in walked June.

"Why, someone looks like he is feeling better." Now, *she* was beaming. Then, after seeing that Zinnia was in the room, she understood why the boy had changed so.

"Young lady, I gave you explicit orders to stay in bed, and here I find you in Peter's room!"

"Oh June, I truly am feeling fine, and I just had to see Peter. He risked his life for me, how could I not?"

"Please, let her stay Aunt June. I love her company and she takes my mind off of my injures." Peter pleaded.

June could not help but smile at their persistence. "Alright, I suppose it would do you both some good." June answered with a little chuckle. "Are either of you hungry?"

"Oh, yes." came Zinnia's quick reply, but from Peter, there only came a low murmured "I guess so."

June hurried down the stairway to prepare two hardy plates of food, while Peter and Zinnia talked. Soon the meals came. Zinnia ate it all, but Peter hardly touched his plate. While Zinnia was eating, Peter told the story of what had happened the previous night to her, June, and Everit.

"Well, Flower and I decided to go on a walk in the woods. The path led us to the river and it really was beautiful, but then all of the sudden, a gray settled upon the sky and the wind blew savagely. We decided we had better get back to the horses, - wait, Everit, Dove is still out by the forest. She is on the road that follows the river. Do you know it?"

"Yes, I will go get her." he said, promptly leaving the room.

Peter continued with his story "Anyhow, I took Flower by the hand and started to run. The rain poured down on us and soon you could scarcely see. Then Flower let go of my hand and started yelling for help. I turned around to go to her, but before a could I heard thunder, and after that, well, I must have passed out. When I came to, I was under a scorched tree that had entrapped my legs. After crawling out from under it, I saw Flower laying in a mud puddle. She was pale and cold. I thought she was dead and that I had failed to save her, but to my relief I found her still breathing. After that I don't remember much, for the only thing on my mind was getting her to safety. I – I guess that is all." Peter finished wearily.

"Oh, Peter!" cried Zinnia with terror. She laid her head on his chest. "I am so sorry for all of the trouble I have put you through-

"No! You mustn't say that! I would do it a thousand times over just to have you here by my side!" the young man said defiantly.

"That was very brave of you, Peter. I am forever thankful that the Lord was watching over you two." trembled June with large tears gathering on the brims of her eyes. "Come, Zinnia. I think we should go downstairs and leave Peter to rest. We will come back soon, dear." she said to Peter.

So, June and Zinnia both went downstairs, and thanked God yet another time for keeping such a blessed boy safe while in the clasps of wickedness.

# *Chapter XVII*

## *Preparations Begin*

June sent letters to Peter and Zinnia's parents, explaining what had happened, as well as, how they were both recovering rapidly and wished to stay. Peter's parents returned the note with urgency, asking all sorts of questions. June tried her best to answer them, and after getting everything straightened out, they agreed to let their boy stay if that was what pleased him.

Zinnia's parents, on the other hand, took a few days to write back and seemed not to mind if Zinnia stayed with June as long as she was happy. Her mother wrote,

*Dear Ms. McCafre,*

*I am sorry to be informed of such a misfortunate event. I am sure, if you say she is well, she is. Tell her we miss her, and that we are thinking of her and the young gentleman who saved her. If there is any change in news, please contact us.*

*Affectionally,*

*Mrs. Eloise Ellis*

June read the letter and nearly shuttered at its formality. She did tell Zinnia that her mother and father were missing her, but she most definitely did not show the girl this unaffectionate letter.

A month went by, and Peter grew better with each coming day. When he caught news that he only needed something as minor as a cast on his right arm, the lad deliberately began braking June's rule of always staying in bed. It did not take long before the young man was insisting upon some household tasks to fill his time.

While Peter *was* stuck in bed, Zinnia had stayed by his side night and day. She lovingly talked to him, and soon she knew almost everything about this once thought of stranger, as did Peter know most everything about his beloved Flower. The pairs' laughter could be heard echoing in the hall for hours, and soon it was evident that they had found in each other a beau.

One day, while June was dicing carrots to put into a soup, Zinnia's eye caught a glimmering sparkle coming from her hand. The girl looked quizzically at the ring for a moment, then she burst forth "June! Where did you get that ring? Did Everit propose?"

June gave a bubbling grin and nodded.

"How could you not tell me? How long have you been engaged? When-"

Just then Peter entered the room. "What is all the commotion about?" asked Peter with a furrowed brow.

"June got engaged and did not have the decency to tell us!" yelled Zinnia.

"Is this true?" Peter asked with and air of excitement.

June nodded once again, which ignited an uproar of questions. After the two calmed down she began to answer them.

"Well, the same night that you two went on your little excursion in the thunderstorm, Everit asked me to marry him-

"What? That long ago?" Zinnia asked passionately.

"Yes, as I was saying, I willing agreed to his proposal. I stayed a while at his house, and then we rode here to tell you both the good news. When I found that neither of you were here, and it began to rain, I started to worry. I would have gone out in the storm myself to find you two, but of course that would have been irrational since I did not know where you had gone. Luckily, Everit stopped me before I made that foolish decision. We waited here until you return and since then, we have been busy bringing you both back to full health. I suppose it simply never crossed our minds to tell you at such a time." June said matter-a-factly.

This explanation did not satisfy Zinnia, but she decided to drop the matter, and instead, rejoice in this momentous occasion. Peter did the same, and soon the questions started again.

Thankfully, Everit came inside. After hearing all of the excitement, he knew what had happened and swooped in to June's rescue. With the couple both trying their hardest to answer Peter and Zinnia's never-ending questions, it seemed many new things had gotten planned.

They were to get married at the end of July, which left very little time for the preparations to remain unfinished. Zinnia went and got a pen, soon she was writing down who was going to be invited to the wedding. June told Zinnia of how she did not want a big deal made out of the day. She only wanted a few people, and to Zinnia that is about all June seemed to know. With the women chattering a mile-a-minute, the men decided their place was outside, and so they went.

After getting a list of names from June, Zinnia immediately started on writing the invitations, while June was making arrangements to go into town to buy her wedding dress.

"Zinnia should we go into town next week for the dress?"

"Town? Oh, June, we can't just take a stroll into town to buy your wedding dress! You only get married once, and I insist upon us going to Louisville for the dress."

"Well, that is quite a big fuss for a little wedding!"

"June, please! I know that I have never planned a wedding before, but I *do* know that a dress is very important. If it is the money that you are worried about, I am sure my mother would be more than happy to pay the expenses. She loves you, and shopping."

"Oh, no dear. It is not the money that worries me. I am sure you are right, but it just seems silly to ride that far for a dress."

"It wouldn't hurt just to look, would it? Please June, I would love to see Louisville again, and it could be like a sort of bride and bridesmaid trip for the two of us. Please?"

"Oh, alright, if it makes you happy." June agreed.

"By the end of this trip, *you* will be the happy one, and by the wedding, Everit will nearly faint at your beauty."

June chuckled and shook her head at the young persistent girl. She had grown to be very proud of her, and she now loved her like a daughter.

The planning went on all day. The men came back inside, but after eating supper Everit gave June a kiss goodbye and went home. Peter stayed up a little while longer before saying "Well, I think I will hit the hay. I am awfully tired from all of this excitement. Good night, Mrs. bride-to-be." Peter called jovially. Then, more affectionately, "Good night, my sweet Flower." he said before retreating to his room. There he did not go to sleep, but instead wrote a letter, and sat in deep thought for hours.

The women stayed downstairs, thinking out every detail of the soon coming wedding. It was past midnight before they went to their bedrooms, though neither of them could sleep once they got there. They were too excited for the glorious celebration of two sweethearts.

# *Chapter XVIII*

# *June and Zinnia Go on a Trip*

The next morning, the whole house was up bright and early. June and Zinnia went about their chores hastily, while Peter was left feeling invalid. Soon, though, Zinnia and June came back into the house and prepared breakfast. They ate, but in silence, for each of them were consumed with their own thoughts.

After finishing their meal, June suggested that Peter and Zinnia go on a walk together. They both were happy to. First, they walked around the buildings, then Zinnia suggested that they walk through the woods. Peter could not refuse her anything and he loved the woods himself, so off they went through the field of wildflowers that surrounded June's forest. Once they were within the solitude of trees, Peter asked "If you do not mind, may I hold your hand while we walk?"

Zinnia blushed, then answered a short "Of course."

So, they walked through the enchanted forest hand in hand. Soon the awkwardness burned away and Zinnia became comfortable once again, which was easy to do since Peter acted so comfortable himself. They strolled by the creek where Zinnia had seen the fawn before, and so she began the conversation.

"I have only been through these woods once, but when I was here, June and I saw a fawn and doe right there near the water. They are such beautiful creatures, don't you think?"

"Yes, I love them myself, all though I know many who would rather hunt them."

"Oh! How awful!" Zinnia shrieked in disgust "I could never imagine breaking up such a glorious family!"

"Yes, I know. Neither could I, but do not worry, your deer are safe in these woods, Flower." Peter asserted.

"So, have you been in these woods much?" Zinnia questioned.

"Yes, I have spent many of my childhood summers playing here."

"Oh, what delightful fun that must have been. I wish I could have come, too."

"Well, you are here now, and I am glad of it." Peter sweetly commented.

"Peter, do you have a favorite tree?"

"I like all of them, but I suppose the tulip tree is my favorite, and you?"

"I have not thought of it much, but yes, I suppose the tulip tree would be mine as well. There was one in the backyard of my old house. I use sit under it quite often just to get away from my parents."

Zinnia had said more than she meant to. There was silence for a moment before Peter asked "What are your parents like?"

"Oh," breathed Zinnia "my father just *loves* business. In fact, that is all he ever thinks about. My family has moved all over the state for him and his silly job, but this last time I decided that I would not move anymore unless I wished to, so here I am.

"My mother stays at home, when she is not off spending money, but she does not do any housework. She actually couldn't if she tried, for she doesn't know the first thing about it. She does whatever Father wants, and only because Father tricks her into liking his way of thinking. She does not do a thing alone, or without someone thinking her next move out for her. It disgusts me, though I still write to her most every week, as I am sure you have realized. I must admit that I did not know much more than her before I came here. I have learned so much. June is a wonderful person, and I am very lucky to have met her. So, what about you? What are your parents like?"

"Well, as I told you, my father owns an orchard. He is busy with that for quite a good portion of the year, but when he isn't, he normally is fixing odds and ends for Mother and the neighbors. He is very handy.

"Mother is a fantastic woman. She cooks and cleans for the whole family, and never gives so much as one complaint. She is always happy to help us with our problems, and has a heart that never runs dry of love. June and her are quite a lot alike.

"I have three younger sisters, of which I love dearly. There is Louisa, who is a lovable young woman of seventeen, she mostly spends her time primping for each sweetheart that comes her way. Clara is sixteen, and she is perfectly satisfied with helping Father work all day, although she tries her very hardest to care about her appearance as much as Louisa. Lastly, there is little May. She is thirteen, and loves to be outside. Mostly she spends her time talking to lilies and climbing trees. Well, that is my whole family."

"I am sure that I would love to meet them someday."

"You will. They will be at the wedding."

"Oh, yes. I had forgotten." Zinnia said, trying to recover from her shock. "I do hope they like me."

"I don't see how they possibly could not." Peter beamed.

Zinnia leaned closer into him as they walked.

"Would you like to see my tulip tree?"

"What? You have a tulip tree?"

"Well, not exactly. It is in this forest, and I sort of claimed it as my own. It is this one." Peter said motioning to a ginormous tree that stood a little off from the trail. "Come with me." he said, while leading Zinnia behind him to the magnificent tree. Then he began to climb it.

"Do you want me to climb it?" questioned Zinnia.

"Yes, you will be safe." Peter answered with an outstretched hand. Zinnia took it and began to climb the tree herself. Once they came to the crown of it, there could be seen hundreds of vibrant leaflets, each stretching their little hands, earnestly trying to touch the golden sun. Zinnia was amazed. She looked over at Peter.

"This is no longer mine, but our tree now." he breathed.

"You don't want to do that; I might ruin it."

"You, my Flower, could only make it more beautiful." Peter said wistfully.

They sat there silently for quite a while, before climbing back down to solid ground. After, Zinnia slipped her hand back into Peter's, they began to walk again. The couple wandered the length of the trail, before going back to the house. June saw them coming hand in hand, and could not help but smile to herself.

A few days later, June and Zinnia where hurrying about trying to get ready for their big trip to Louisville. Everit had come over, just as usual, to see his beloved fiancé off. Peter got their carriage ready, and chose Nickel and Clove for their team. After bringing them down the hill, hitching them to the carriage, and tying them to a post, he said to the women "Your chariot awaits." With a gesture of his hand, he led the way. Everit helped June to her seat, and Peter helped Zinnia.

"Goodbye, my love. Good luck!" Everit said tenderly.

"Goodbye, darling." June said, bubbling over with joy.

"Flower," Peter started.

"Yes?"

"I hope you have a wonderful time. I will miss you."

"Oh Peter, I will miss you too, and I am sure that June and I will have a simply sensational time! Goodbye!" Zinnia called, as June started to drive the carriage away.

"Goodbye." Peter sighed.

After the women had left, Peter walked over to Everit.

Everit muttered "I am sure going to miss them."

"Yes, as will I. They are marvelous to have around. You have chosen for yourself a miraculous wife."

"Why, thank you very much. I think she is quite special myself." Everit said with his steel colored eyes shining.

"Everit, I am sorry to leave you all alone, but I have some business that I must attend to. I will be back before June and Zinnia return, but please, let's keep this between us. I am arranging sort of a- surprise."

"Oh, that's fine. I understand." Everit said with a wink, though Peter truly doubted he did. "It might actually be nice to have some peace and quiet before the "big day". Those women have been talking non-stop, though I must admit, it doesn't bother me much."

"Thanks for understanding. Goodbye."

With that, Peter ran to the house. Once he got there, he dashed up the stairway and into Zinnia's room, where he found an opened letter on her desk. Glancing at the envelope, he scribbled a few digits on a scrap piece of paper, and then sped out the door and to the barn to get his horse. From there, he rode like mad till he came to the nearest town, and there he took a train that was headed towards Elkhart.

Later that same evening, Peter returned home smiling radiantly. He was in a wonderful mood, and was genial to everyone and thing. He put his horse back in its stable, and caroled joyously back down the hill. He did a little jig when his feet touched the porch step, then wandered up to his room and hid what he had gotten from his journey. After stumbling numbly back down the stairs, he went to the front porch to wait for June and Zinnia. Though he did not have to wait long, for once he stepped out the door, he saw dust flying and a carefully moving carriage coming towards the house. It was June and Zinnia. When Peter walked up to their carriage, he saw that each of them seemed to be completely dazed with happiness.

"Hello, my ladies. How was your excursion?" Peter questioned winningly.

"Oh, it was heavenly." breathed Zinnia.

"Yes, I had a delightful time. Thank you for taking me, darling." June said sweetly to Zinnia. Then she stated "Peter, we have quite a lot to unload. Would you be a dear and help us?"

"Of course, Aunt June."

There truly was a pile in the back of that carriage. Peter carried each package into June's bedroom, where he delicately stacked them on her bed. June and Zinnia went inside, and attempted to calm themselves from such an exciting journey.

"Boy, I did not know that it was possible to buy so much in just one day." Peter said impressed.

"It was difficult, but as you can see, we managed." joked Zinnia merrily.

"I will go put the carriage and horses in the barn, then I suppose we should go tell Everit you are here."

"Oh, yes!" cried June as if she had forgotten.

Peter did as he said, and then all three of them rode over to see Everit. They found him outside resting under his large pine tree.

"Hello, darling!" caroled June.

"Hello, my love. I did not know you had returned."

"Yes, we just got home."

"Was the trip successful?"

"My, but it was!" cried June, acting like a disquieted child.

"Remember," admonished Zinnia "don't tell him anything. It is to be a surprise. You understand, don't you Everit?" Zinnia asked with a charming grin.

"Of course." he answered knowingly.

"I will make us supper." declared June.

"No, us men will make supper tonight. That is, if you are willing to help me, Peter."

"Sure." Peter quickly answered.

"What are you two chefs making us tonight?" questioned Zinnia playfully.

"Well, tonight I believe we are going to have smoked trout, but first, Peter and I will have to go out and catch them."

"That sounds delightful." asserted June.

"Yes, and it will give June and I plenty of time to take our well-deserved nap. When shall we come back over?" Zinnia asked.

"Oh, say six-thirty."

"Great! Goodbye men!" Zinnia said with a wave of her rosy hand.

June and Zinnia left to take their nap, while Everit gathered the necessary tools to catch their supper. Once everything was packed into a pail, Peter and Everit walked to the nearby stream. There they fished for about an hour, and caught more than an ample amount of fish for the meal. After toting the heavy bucket back to the house, Peter began to fillet the colorful fish and Everit started to prepare the fire. All in all, everything went swimmingly, but of course, it was not quite a simple task for the two untrained cooks. The meal was finished just in the nick of time. It was full of such bold and admirable flavors that even the women were greatly impressed. What a sweet and loving jester it truly was. Nothing could have been appreciated more by the two well-honored women.

After finishing the meal and playing a few games of cards, Peter, Zinnia, and June left Everit's house, and rode back to their own. There they talked about the events of the day, and laughed with pleasant exhaustion. Soon it was time to go to bed, and so they did, in hopes to have a successful day of work in the soon arriving morrow.

# *Chapter XIX*

# *Two New Beginnings*

Throughout the coming weeks many things were done, and with very little time to do them. Peter and Zinnia worked vigorously on decorating the backyard with various wildflowers and ferns, while June cleaned the house and looked through her mother's old recipes for something delicious to cook for the wedding.

Soon, the day came in which June was going to be married. Peter and Zinnia were busy sprucing up the outdoors with bunches of freshly cut prairie grasses and vibrant bouquets of bleeding-hearts, which had been beautifully preserved, through the heat of summer, in their cool moist swampy home. June had cooked nearly all of the food the day prior, so, at least, she did not have that to worry about. Instead, she was upstairs in Zinnia's room being fussed over and made-up. Zinnia had finished adding blush to June's cheeks, and had quickly set to work on her hair. She braided it into a long rope that ran down June's back. At the bottom of her hair, she curled the end bits that did not fit into the braid, then she took lovely little flowers and tucked them randomly throughout June's hair. At the top of her head, where the braid began, Zinnia arranged a halo of ferns and elegant flowers until June looked like Mother Nature herself. Then Zinnia went about helping June into her dress. It was such a beautiful dress indeed, for although plain, it was dainty and very becoming. The dress fit June as if it were made just for her. It was of standard white, but then it had satin and sheer layers that alternated throughout the dress making it wonderfully interesting. The sleeves fell down around the elbows, and the neckline gently hugged her throat. Once June had finished dressing, she appeared lovelier than an angel.

People had started to arrive, and the ceremony was about to begin, before Zinnia had even begun dressing or fixing her hair. Everyone was seated in the backyard that overlooked the wildflower field. Their seats were white with ribbons and flowers streaming from the back. There was a mossy pathway, which ran in-between these seats, that led to a bower which was enclosed with deeply blooming, purple wisteria. The woodland's flowers and ferns lined and completed this picture with all of their glory. Each guest that arrived was in shock by the magnificent scene that lay before them.

June and Zinnia, both, were growing excited. Soon, a low buzz could be heard from the people below. Zinnia could depict the neighbors that June and herself had visited only months before, as well as all of their children, who obediently sat in their chairs and behaved with grace.

Peter came and told them that they were ready. First Zinnia exited the house, she was wearing a silvery green dress that had a few little flower shaped diamonds scattered across it. This dress reached her elbows and had a neckline that met her collar bone. Her hair was curled, and then pinned back to show her radiant face.

Zinnia walked to her position at the front of the aisle where she met Peter. At seeing her, Peter's knees began to shake. She was lovelier than any sight he had ever seen, and soon his mind became so dazed that he no longer could remember anything but her beauty. Luckily, Zinnia took his arm, and together they strolled down the aisle, smiling all the way. Once they came to the bower, they split apart and went to opposite sides. Everit was there, anxiously awaiting June's coming. When they were settled into their positions, they looked back down the aisle and saw June. She was blushing and smiling widely as she walked towards them. Everyone gasped at her loveliness, and each eye in the crowd was full of tears.

The ceremony began, and within a few heavenly moments, June and Everit were married. Then began the celebration. Everyone piled into the house, and immediately loud rapturous talking began. There was ample food for everyone, and each ate hardily. The food was savory and irresistible, so it was quickly demolished.

At this time, Zinnia met Peter's family. They were just as he had described them. His father was a kind man with blue eyes, just as Peter's. He was very reserved, yet still it seemed you knew exactly how he felt. His mother was a plump woman, with rosy cheeks and shining eyes. No one could have been sweeter. She talked to Zinnia as if she had known her for her entire life, and most definitely was not shy in showing her affection. Peter's sisters were equally genial, and all seemed to love her, especially May, whose loving eyes were transfixed on Zinnia's every movement.

Next, they all went to the backyard were one of the neighbors began to play his fiddle. Soon, everyone was dancing and twirling about the yard in one joyous motion. Peter took Zinnia by the hand and began to tenderly dance with her, but soon the song changed and they were moving so fast that neither of them could hardly breathe. Peter's parents saw how their boy admired Zinnia, and thought it a lovely thing. It truly was a wonderful night.

People began to give June and Everit their best wishes, and then slowly left. The seats were emptying, and soon began the overwhelming task of cleaning up the mess. Everit and June quickly changed into more comfortable attire, grabbed their bags, and set off for their honeymoon. They were to travel to Colorado and see the mountains for the first time. Everit had always meant to make this journey, and now he would, but even better, he was now to make it with the love of his life.

"Thank you for everything you two!" cried June happily to Peter and Zinnia.

"Oh, it was our pleasure!" beamed Zinnia "Have fun!"

"We will! I love you two! Goodbye! We will be back soon!"

"Goodbye!" Peter and Zinnia both called in unison.

It was a perfect day from start to finish, but it was not finished yet.

"Well," sighed Zinnia "I had better get into more fitting attire."

"Of course, I will meet you here." Peter said cordially.

Zinnia walked up to the vacant house, and went to her room. To her surprise, there was a leaf on her desk, but not just any leaf, a tulip tree leaf. On it there was etched a note. This is what it read;

*My Dearest Flower,*

*Please come, and meet me at our tree as soon as possible.*

*I will be waiting for you.*

*-Peter*

Zinnia did not understand what this letter meant. Obviously, she should follow the directions, and so she did, but it was a great mystery indeed to her.

She briskly walked outside, then to the forest's entry. After following the trail for a time, Peter came into sight. He was waiting for her, just as he had promised. Once she came to him, she began to ask a question, but before she could finish, she was stopped by the odd look on Peter's face. He stood there, tall and strong, his eyes gleaming in the moonlight. Those beautiful eyes seemed to only see Zinnia; who was still in her shimmering dress, with her delicate face full of wonder. Once Peter caught his breath, he began to speak.

"Flower, there is something I have been meaning to tell you. It is the reason I asked you here. You see, I am in love with you. So madly in love, that I can hardly think straight. I have loved you ever since the day I met you in the barn, and I know I will go right on loving you until this world's end. You are the most beautiful thing that has ever stepped foot on this earth, and I just wanted to ask, Zinnia Ellis, will you marry me?" Peter bent down on one knee, and revealed a dazzling emerald ring. There he bowed to her, and awaited his answer.

Zinnia stood there, with moonbeams dancing across her face, in utter silence. Then with a passionate whisper she answered "Of course, I will Peter. I love you."

That was all Peter needed to know before he gave her an ardent kiss. Then the lad, with heart blazing, carried his dumb-founded Flower to the house, were he gently laid her on the sofa.

"Flower, my love, say something." he breathed.

"Oh, Peter!" she cried "I am so happy! I have loved you since the first time we met, and I could have never imagined that you would love me back!"

"Why? As I said, you are the most beautiful thing that has ever walked the earth." Peter asserted without a doubt.

"Peter, you amaze me!" smiled Zinnia, nearly bubbling over with joy. "It is only that I never could have dreamt that my life would end up so altogether lovely."

"Well, my Flower, as Aunt June always says, "that is the beauty of one's journey."

Made in the USA
Monee, IL
04 July 2021